LEAH ORR
#1 Amazon Bestselling Author of The She Shed
The
Retirees

Pre-release Praise from Readers with Advance Reader Copies
The Retirees

"An entertaining read filled with humor, camaraderie, and just enough suspense to keep readers turning the pages." - *Kirkus Reviews*

"*The Retirees* celebrates chaos, absurdity, and courage in life's final act, proving that growing old can still mean raising a little hell." - Publishers Weekly/Book Life.

An American "Thursday Murder Club" with a twist! - K.Siddall

Believable characters and a plot that makes this cozy mystery a bit more deadly and unputdownable. - K. Simmons

Orr's sharp dialogue and quirky characters make every page sparkle with charm and unexpected depth. It's like *The Golden Girls* met *Murder, She Wrote* and decided to raise a little hell. A. Sanders

If Bette Davis was right when she said, "Old age ain't no place for sissies," Orr takes it a step further: old age might just be the best place to stir trouble, crack mysteries, and live more boldly than ever. The Retirees don't just redefine retirement — they reclaim it as a stage where life's most surprising adventures can unfold. - P. Parker

Retirement goals: Morning boozy coffees, chasing down cold cases, themed parties, and Mr Anderson. The next phase of life does not get better than this. Every character becomes your friend. You will love the twist at the end. A must-read! - L. Unger

The book is filled with surprise twists & turns along with an abundance of warmhearted humor that keeps you engrossed until the very end! Who knew that retirement could be this much fun! - D. Bleiler

Welcome to The Ocean's Edge, where the cocktail coffees are strong, the secrets run deep, and Mr. Anderson, the cat, knows every detail of the murders that happen before happy hour - J. O'Neil

Pour yourself a spiked coffee, grab a slice of sugar cream pie, and settle in because murder has never been this much fun. - M.Baker

This book is printed in the USA.
Distributed by IngramSpark/Lightning Source LLC
Published Jan 5, 2026

The Library of Congress Control Number: 2025915939

First Edition
ISBN Paperback 9798991042031
ISBN Hardcover 9798991042048
ISBN Ebook   9798991042055

Leah Orr
Jensen Beach, Florida

In a book club? Want signed copies?
Contact Leah directly at:
www.leahorr.com
Or by email:
orrplace1@bellsouth.net

Dedicated to my mom, Josie, who passed away before I completed this story. She would have adored every one of these characters.

Dear readers,

Because I often receive emails from fans who enjoy my novels but don't care for some of the language within, I cleaned this story up just for you. Until then . . . fuck, fuckity, fuck, fuck, fuck . . .
Here we go . . .

The Retirees

Leah Orr

Old age is no place for sissies.
- Bette Davis

Prologue

Mr. Anderson

Disco is dead—not just musically or lyrically. Disco is *actually* dead. To be fair, disco did make a comeback for a time. Musicians and DJs enjoyed mixing seventies and eighties melodies with a hacked mash-up of manufactured noises, mumbo jumbo, or whatever they pawn off as music these days. They'd add vocals, edit with computer programs, and label it retro.

Disco is dead—literally. Centered in the clubhouse ceiling, a thirty-inch disco ball hangs delightfully, ready to dazzle all who enter as light dances across the round styrofoam spectacle. The tiny mirrored squares reflect light, creating shimmering art along the walls as the sun rises through the floor-to-ceiling windows. The elderly residents revere this flamboyant orb like the Romans revered Venus, the Goddess of Love, every first Saturday of the month. That's when the disco dance shindig kicks off, but if you ask me, these coffin dodgers would dance until dawn beneath this stupid silver sphere every day that ends with the letter *y* if their bodies would allow.

A bloody butcher knife protrudes from the right side of the silvery globe as blood pools below. Blood flows slowly from the dead body beneath it, like a tiny river, toward the front entrance. Home builders in South Florida cut every corner to save a dollar, so you won't find an establishment with level flooring south of Orlando. The body lies dead on the dance floor, eyes wide open, staring up toward the mirrored ball dangling from above. Even in death, the body continues to worship that giant glittery meatball.

I could captivate you with a story about how this all came to be. I'd love to share it with you. I'm always the first to stumble upon the deceased. I'd be eager to explain everything to the police in meticulous detail when they arrive. I'm perceptive, hypervigilant, and a perfectionist. I notice everything but say nothing. Like wallpaper or antique furniture, no one fully recognizes my charm, character, or priceless value. This group of mismatched septuagenarians pays little attention to me. They're self-absorbed and enamored by boring, trifling bits of bygone eras. So I generally keep to myself. Occasionally, someone will offer a "Hello" or "How are you today?" It's mostly small talk. Often, I don't bother answering their questions. Most mornings, I hold my head high and concentrate on my morning routine, striding by and settling down by the window to watch the hummingbirds enjoy their breakfast nectar at the feeder.

My name is Roger, but I'm known around here as Mr. Anderson. That's what they call me, anyway.

To fully understand my story in the present, it's essential to update you about my past. My mom gave me up when I was barely six weeks old, and an old man named Monty took me in and cared for me. I grew up feeling happy and loved. Recently, he passed away from what the police described as natural causes. I'm skeptical about that. Let's put a pin in this for now. We'll come back to it later.

More about me. I have a few friends—well, only one, actually. Her name is Carol, and she's the nurse here at The Ocean's Edge. Sometimes she sits beside me and shares stories about the cakes and pies she helped bake when her mom owned a pastry shop in Jensen Beach. I love her as much as I adore Key lime pie. The others tend to shy away from me when I pass by, ignoring me as though I have nothing important to offer. That's simply not the case. I'm a good listener and a great companion. Heck, I was a brave sailor and navigator of the often treacherous Florida seas in my youth.

Nevertheless, I've lived here for nearly sixteen years, longer than most of these kooks. I'm much more than just a spectator; I'm a music enthusiast. I enjoy music that evokes emotions—love, heartbreak, or bliss. I've come to appreciate their fascination with Frank Sinatra and Cher; after all, they are legends. I genuinely believe in doing things "My Way," and I believe there is "life after love." However, some of the Motown funk that these folks enjoy feels too dated for me. I don't understand why some old-timers remain so stuck in the past.

Taylor Swift is my favorite artist. I truly admire a self-made woman. She's folksy, she's pop, and she writes her own music. Her lyrics are relevant and resonate with the moment. She might even be more talented than—dare I say—Diana Ross or Donna Summer. For the record, I'm also a big fan of Michael Jackson's musical talent. However, I can no longer idolize him—you know why.

Over time, I've come to recognize that people often return to the moments in their lives when they were happiest, and music from that era elicits all those significant, primal feelings: joy, freedom, and happiness.

I'm the curious type, although I fully understand that curiosity kills. I've got countless secrets I could share. I know where all the proverbial bodies are buried. However, no one cares to listen, mainly because they're too wrapped up in neighborhood tittle-tattle or their mysterious geriatric ailments that seem to multiply daily. Most likely, it's because no one at The Ocean's Edge can fully comprehend my language. And for the most part, I understand their apprehension. Why would any of these old geezers take the time to get to know *me*? I'm just a cat.

Several Months Earlier

Chapter One

Diana
Axed

Starting over is never easy. Don't let anyone tell you otherwise. You create a life for yourself, and then, one day, unexpectedly, it all goes tits up. My fifth husband's death was no surprise—and honestly, good riddance—but getting axed from the executive board of Florida's largest sugar company, which my grandfather built and where I grew exponentially, was painful. However, painful doesn't fully capture how my body churns and rots within. Agony. That's a better word. I'd rather relive the deaths or disposal of every husband than relive the moment they let me go.

"It's time, Diana." My daughter, Lola, nods confidently in my direction. "You've accomplished a lot." She's trying to placate me. "We are all eternally grateful for your contributions over the years, but it's time for this company to move on in a different direction, and we've got to let you go." Yada yada.

I didn't absorb any further bullshit after the words "We've got to let you go." A devilish grin creeps across Lola's face as she looks around at the other board members seated around the conference table. The board members dart their eyes back from me to her. Their soulless eyes wait intently for me to shatter. I won't allow them the satisfaction.

My grandfather built this twenty-seat mahogany table with his own hands. I find myself staring down at it as if this piece of furniture has betrayed me or, rather, as if I expected it to magically grow arms, reach up, embrace me, and somehow save me in this moment—the mind behaves in peculiar ways. I find myself clenching my fists in anger. I'm reminded of my grandfather's advice in the early days of my career: They can't crucify you if your hands are in fists.

The board members nod in unison, grinning back at her and diverting their eyes from me to her. She's enjoying this! I can almost feel the jubilance radiating from her skin. It's as if she has been waiting years for this moment, and finally . . . the day has arrived. She's smitten with herself.

I envision her celebrating with a bottle of cabernet later this evening with her beautiful husband on their veranda at sunset. This vision disgusts me, not because she's reveling in my demise at her behest but rather because she chose such an exquisite man to spend her life with. So what if I'm jealous? Still, I will take credit for raising a confident, intelligent woman who has excellent taste in men. What is it they say? Your only wish for your children is for them to make better choices than your own?

I don't call for a vote, even though they are required to do so formally. I won't endure that kind of humiliation, especially at the hands of my own daughter.

Truth be told, I don't blame her one bit. She takes no prisoners. She's ruthless, like I was at her age, and I admire her ability to set family aside. "Business First" has always been the family motto. "Sugar is thicker than blood" was my grandfather's favorite expression. He was a bastard, but he was also brilliant, wealthy, and well-respected.

I agreed to resign with an impressive severance package that the lawyers painstakingly squabbled over for nearly three months. In the end, I was compensated fairly. I give myself an imaginary pat on the back. Luckily, I've always been a fierce negotiator.

I still own 49 percent of the company, but I no longer have a say in its operations. The global sugar market is expected to increase by nearly two hundred million tons this year alone and is projected to grow by 6.5 percent year-over-year through 2030. The company requires fresh, young visionaries on the board to expand future growth.

It's still agonizing to be discarded like last week's wilted kale. Who am I kidding? I don't eat kale. Not much makes sense anymore.

I don't scream or obsess over the tangled wreckage of my life. Instead, at seventy-four years young, I choose to pursue a fresh start. I'm fine. Really. I suppose. More or less. All things considered.

Like many women my age, I decided to sell my home, a few cars, and a smattering of furniture. I gave away some haggard, unwanted possessions to the pickers on Facebook Marketplace. People will take just about anything for free these days. That's how I ended up here at The Ocean's Edge.

The Ocean's Edge is a fifty-five plus community beautifully nestled along Florida's Treasure Coast. Its website promotes it as an idyllic mixed-use community featuring townhomes, condos, and single-family homes that share a clubhouse, dance studio, yoga studio, movie theater, two restaurants (one poolside and one beachside), a small but efficient medical clinic, and a marina.

Photographs and illustrations showcase homes and common areas featuring immaculately manicured deep-green lawns that are uniformly mowed. Flower beds overflow with a striking mix of blooms in vibrant reds, yellows, and purples. Flowering trees are thoughtfully placed to provide exquisitely designed focal points throughout the campus.

All of this creates a perfect studio backdrop for a Hallmark or Netflix midsummer murder mystery drama. The only caveat is the proximity of the cemetery in the adjacent lot. It's like nature's way of saying "No rush, but . . . you won't have to move far." The presence of the dead residing so close gives me the shivers. It's pretty funny though, when you think about it. It's like the ultimate senior living package: independent living, assisted living, then . . . permanent residence.

I never imagined I would live in a retirement community. I envisioned my retirement in a quaint cottage by the ocean on the west coast of Florida with the man of my dreams. Unfortunately, my life didn't turn out that way, as the five poor choices in men I made are long gone, either dead or discarded. However, it's never too late in life to find a new boy toy. If Madonna and Cher could enjoy a young stud in life's final encore, so could I.

Chapter Two

Diana
The Arrival

On the seventh day of January 2025, my driver, Jeb, escorts me out of my Bentley. There's no better time than the start of a new year to embark upon a new life adventure. Inspired by Demi Moore winning a Golden Globe for her role in *The Substance* at age sixty-two, I remind myself that I'm never too old to explore new experiences or take on a new *role*, to fit the metaphor adequately.

I didn't forward my address. The best part about not forwarding my old address is that I will no longer receive junk mail from my dirtbag ex-husbands—a constant reminder of poor decisions. This year, 2025, will be a year of new beginnings.

Today is Tuesday. I don't like Mondays. Never start anything new on a Monday, or it's destined for failure. That's my advice—take it! Healthy diets and exercise routines often kick off on Mondays and rarely end well. Just ask anyone!

Sticking with the theme of bringing everything new into the new year, today I'm dressed from head to toe in all new clothing and accessories. I feel empowered by my new red midi dress with bell sleeves, black sandals, a new black leather Dooney & Bourke handbag, hoop earrings, and black lace unmentionables. New clothes are empowering, but new lingerie makes you feel fierce, sultry, and unstoppable.

At the grand entrance, twenty-foot mahogany doors welcome me, and a tall, distinguished gentleman nearing a suitable retirement age offers a wide smile in my direction.

"Hello, and welcome to The Ocean's Edge," he hails in a bubbly voice, extending his right arm and gesturing for me to come inside. He introduces himself, but I don't catch his name, and I don't care. He rambles on about the architecture and design of the main campus. I'm not intrigued by a chatterbox spewing unnecessary information and pointless details about such things that I couldn't care less about. I read the brochure. I'm too old for drab conversations and nonsense.

I interrupt him mid-pitch. "I'm Diana." I extend my hand to shake his, asserting confidence and control. "I've already made my decision to live here.

I'm moving into a townhouse at 60 Crane Lane," I say flatly. I reach into my purse and hand over an envelope containing the closing documents, eager to fulfill this task so I can get past the formalities and move on with my life. It's been a long day, a terrible past few months, and a hellish year.

"Yes, Diana. We've been expecting you. Please, come this way." He gestures for me to follow him into the country club.

Four people at a round table greet me with a flurry of pleasantries: hello, welcome, good morning, and please join us for coffee, won't you?

"Thank you for the invitation, but I have the movers here and need to escort them to my new home."

"Tomorrow, then?" one man asks.

"We meet around eight a.m. every morning for coffee," adds the other, much larger man.

"Please join us," twin Asian women say in unison.

"Um, alright then, why not?" I agree, somewhat reluctantly. "I'm Diana." I wave my hand. In real life, outside the boardroom, people greet potential friends with a wave. No one shakes hands anymore, especially after Covid. I'm not ready to touch so many new people yet, so just a little wave will do for now. New surroundings . . . one step at a time.

"Yes, we've heard *quite a bit* about you." The
smaller man pauses, snapping his fingers as he tries to
remember something. "Oh, that's right, they call you
the sugar heiress," he says.

"You've heard a lot about me?" I'm taken aback
for a moment because I wasn't expecting the
attention. "For the record, I was known as the sugar
queen. My daughter, Lola, is currently the sugar
queen and new *heiress*."

"Yes. I heard your heiress daughter urged you to
enjoy an early retirement. Apparently, the seventies
are *not* the new forties in the business world," blurts
the smaller, wiry, athletic mix of an ex-surfer and a
hippie stoner, unable to hold back.

"Oh, good grief!" One of the Asian women elbows
the man in the ribs. I notice that he has a glass eye.
The way the light hits it reminds me of a blue topaz
bracelet my third husband gifted me for Valentine's
Day many years ago. A blue bracelet for a red-themed
holiday highlights his lack of attention to detail—one
of many reasons I ended things as I did. It's funny
how such small details can trigger the past to seep in
uninvited. I blink the memory away swiftly. Life's too
short to linger in painful places. Anyway, the man's
glass eye is the same shade of blue as his Hawaiian
shirt, which is visually appealing. I admire a man who

can coordinate clothing with accessories. I'll be sure to ask about his backstory. I love a dramatic tale, especially those that end with a missing limb, appendage, or major organ. His eye, however, is not nearly as interesting as his silver-streaked man bun, which is quite large. The man bun was popular for a time, but it's no longer in fashion. Nevertheless, he wears it well.

"Sorry about Bill. He tends to say whatever rubbish pops into his mind without first filtering his thoughts for polite company. I'm Filomena." The woman pats her chest and glares at Bill. "Who says the seventies are the new forties? I've never heard that before." She taps her chin and adds, "However, Cher and Dolly Parton look just as stunning as they did in their forties."

"Maybe in Hollywood, with plastic surgery, facelifts, butt lifts, and a vaginal makeover," says the other Asian woman who looks just like Filomena. They wear matching purple cat eyeglasses that are slightly oversized for their faces. Both have haircuts reminiscent of Uma Thurman in Quentin Tarantino's iconic 1994 dark comedy thriller, *Pulp Fiction*. "I'm Estelle, Filomena's sister."

"That's quite alright, ladies. I appreciate you defending me, but I was born in the Everglades, and

I've wrangled a reptile or two in my day," I say, determined to stand my ground. "Yes, it's true, Bill. I *was* let go. It was time for me to retire anyway. I look forward to this next chapter in my life, truth be told. And since you already seem to know quite a bit about me, let me share something you may or may not already know." I let out a big sigh, feeling a bit persnickety today, stressed about the move and my forced retirement, of course. "I may look like Paula Deen, the culinary genius of confectionary delights, but my name is Diana. I'm well aware of the reputation surrounding my legacy. They call me Lady Di, but not like Princess Diana. Lady D-I-E because sugar kills."

"Heavens to Betsy. That's harsh," says Estelle, radiating sympathy.

"It's true, sadly. Sugar kills not only when ingested, but it also contaminates the waters, the soil, and the air we breathe. That's just the beginning, not to mention its impact on your metabolism. I've become more of an environmentalist lately; I was trying to guide the company toward a more responsible, sustainable direction, harming fewer fish, wildlife, and people in the process. And . . . well . . . they fired me. They can eff off for all I care." I throw my hands up in despair, reflecting on the disastrous last few months I've experienced. It actually feels good to release some of my pent-up anger.

"Oh, let me stop you right there for a moment," says the large, perhaps 275-pound, brawny, bald gentleman with broad, rigid shoulders. "The HOA doesn't permit swearing around here. You'll be fined a public nuisance fee for disturbing the peace."

"Good Lord! That's a load of malarkey, and just to clarify, I didn't actually say the f-word in its entirety," I exclaim.

"It was not my intention to upset you. I'm glad you're here. I'm Dennis. Dennis Duncan. I'm a retired detective. Nice to meet you." He scoots away from the table, stands up, and extends his hand for a handshake, so I'm forced to follow his lead. His grip is firm. I appreciate a man with a firm handshake. Forceful. Strong.

"I know you didn't say the f-word," Filomena explains. "I'm sure Dennis wanted to enlighten you straight away about one of the many zany rules around here. You'll get used to it. We've come up with a few other creative words that will suffice. It's actually fun; it's like creating a new language. Meet with us tomorrow morning once you're settled, and we'll give you the four-one-one on everything Ocean's Edge." Filomena raises her eyebrows and widens her eyes, and I can tell she's got some interesting tea to spill.

"Sounds scandalous," I say sarcastically.

"A word of advice," Bill warns. "Beware of Tom, that sanctimonious sloth who greeted you at the entrance. He's insufferable. Avoid him at all costs. He can talk the face off a clock." He drums the table with his fingertips, then adds, "Oh, and steer clear of Nurse Carol too. She's always trying to jab us with some new poison or government-mandated concoction under the pretense of keeping us alive to witness another sunset."

"Oh, brother, don't mind Bill and his mostly entertaining but sometimes wackadoodle conspiracies. We're so glad to have you, Diana. You're going to love it here," insists Filomena.

"Sure as sh—" I start to say but catch myself before finishing the word. "I mean, sure as sugar," I blurt out before giving a "toodle-oo" as I turn and walk away.

In the distance, as I vacate the clubhouse, I hear the gossip and chatter starting up already. She's a real dynamo, that one . . . an iron-willed sugar momma . . . the queen bee of the sugar sea . . . she's going to fit in here just fine . . . I'm going to call her sugar tits (for sure, that comment came from one-eyed Bill). All this

attention brings a cheerful smile to my face,
something I haven't enjoyed in quite some time.

Chapter Three

Theo

Have you ever wondered what it would feel like to stab someone in the eye? Or gut someone just above the belt? Would the knife skewer the eye? Or would it pop out of the socket and bounce along across the kitchen linoleum? Would intestines slither out once the belly is slit open? I wonder about such things often. Unfortunately, I can't offer any valuable insight because it's not my typical MO, modus operandi, as they say in all those detective shows people love to binge-watch these days. Murder. Now *that* I know well. I can tell you how *that* feels.

I'd have to say it feels divinely delightful.

Initially, you feel a surge of adrenaline as your heart races, followed by a soothing release of endorphins during the act. Then a sense of calm washes over you like a gentle wave of serenity. Generally, I feel powerful and important. I have just made the world a better place. The world needs me.

Am I a good person or a bad person? I see myself as the hero of my story, while others might view me as a villain.

Seventeen Green Street. That was my home. No. That's a lie. The word *home* implies family. Family infers love. There was no love in that home.

I was born bad—a bad seed, as some people say. Never good from day one. Just ask my mom. I never slept, always cried, and so on. Only you can't ask my mom. She's dead. Death by shellfish in a fancy restaurant—a ridiculous way to die. Irresponsible. Her date told the police he didn't know she had an allergy, and the waitstaff didn't ask about food restrictions back then. Halfway through her Caesar salad, which contained dressing with anchovies, she collapsed onto the red-and-black marbled floor before the ambulance could arrive.

She dated numerous men in those days, after my father passed. She blamed me for his death and also berated me for having to date so many men, hoping to find a new husband who would be willing to help raise me. It was all *my fault*. Everything was always *my fault*. Well, Mom, sorry this date didn't turn out so well for you.

After her passing, my uncle raised me in Connecticut. I attended a prestigious high school and received the best Ivy League college education money could buy.

Sadly, wherever I go, tragedy follows. Much like in literary fiction, every grand adventure or heartwarming love story portends a tragedy to follow.

Most people who commit murder never genuinely intend to take a life. Often, murder results from unintended consequences. Of course, there are instances when individuals consider killing others. Who hasn't had that thought? It's a natural human emotion, but few actually follow through with it.

I've killed more than a few people, but unlike most murderers, I fully intended to kill them. I stalked them and planned diligently. Upon reflection, in my old but not quite elderly years, I wish I hadn't. Don't get me wrong; they had it coming. Still, they had families and people who loved them, people who thought they knew them. They didn't. The world is better off without them. I should be relieved, but murder is brutal to live with—a mark upon your soul that's never forgiven or forgotten.

I can't tell you my name. I could make one up—something clever—to move the story along, but quite frankly, I'm not that creative, and what's the point, really? Eventually, I'll be caught and killed or, worse, imprisoned. Scratch that. Call me Theo. It means "gift from God" in Greek. Theo seems fitting.

I'm clever. I've evaded the police for so many years that I'm fortunate to have ended up in such a lovely fifty-five plus community like The Ocean's Edge. Who would have thought that all these years would pass without any genuine leads pointing the cops in my direction? So much so that I could live out my days in Florida, in a posh paradise, with the money I confiscated and the freedom I unjustly claimed for myself. I should enjoy it, but guilt has a way of dampening joy.

For now, I try not to get too attached to people or make too much of a fuss about anything at all. I read a lot, mostly nonfiction self-help books about how to be happy, like *The Art of Happiness* by the illustrious Dalai Lama, *The Happiness Project* by Gretchen Rubin, and most recently, *The Let Them Theory* by Mel Robbins. Like everyone else, my life is a work in progress. I can be better and do better. It's never too late to reinvent myself.

Today I bask in the sun at the ocean's shore, reading a book, trying to savor the peace of this time in my life. I hope to outlast my past indiscretions and wish that one day, my secrets will be buried along with me. I make an effort to surround myself with kind, good people so I don't feel compelled to harm anyone else. I'm tired. I'm growing older. I want to lay down my sword, so to speak. I want to enjoy my retirement in peace and luxury. But sadly, a vigilante never rests.

Chapter Four

Diana
Joining the Team

7:15 a.m. arrives quickly, and the sun brightens my bedroom, reminding me that I desperately need curtains. In hindsight, choosing a townhouse with an east-facing bedroom window was not the optimal choice. I reach for my phone on the nightstand and ask Siri to remind me to call Rebecca, my assistant, this afternoon. I need to get an interior designer here right away. Rebecca was part of my severance package. She's the best perk I won in the bargaining game—a reward to help me transition to a new life. While I also secured the Bentley and my driver, Jeb, Rebecca was my finest acquisition.

After my forced retirement, I ditched nearly all of my clothing. I'll never have to wear a suit again. My daughter assured me that retired living casual wear is very chic and relaxing. It's easy, she said. Just dress like you're on a cruise ship. She suggested I Google boho dresses and pants online, and I'd have lots of choices. She wasn't wrong. I chose a few designs I admired, and Rebecca had my dressmaker prepare a wardrobe I could be proud of.

Feeling refreshed from a good night's rest in my new townhome, free from the sun's intrusion, I decide to accept the residents' invitation and stroll over to the country club for a cup of coffee. The weather is cool today, so cruise wear will have to wait, which is fine because I tend to feel warm these days with hot flashes, making the cool air feel pleasant.

A small voice inside my head suggests maybe a red sweater today, while another suggests the black one. A third suggests, Don't overthink it, Diana. A simple blouse with a jacket to keep yourself warm will do just fine. It's funny how the voices inside your head speak louder once you're retired and live alone. It's as if they know you're lonely and could use a little company—so they suddenly have more to say.

I settle upon a red V-neck sweater, jeans, and tan sheepskin boots. It's a cute outfit, warm, stylish—not too fuddy-duddy, not too hotsy-totsy. I quickly unwind the curlers from my hair, brush out the curls, brush my teeth, and apply a bit of makeup before rushing out the door.

A mere few seconds pass after I enter the room before one-eyed Bill bellows, "I told you she would come."

Dennis, the retired detective, slides a one-dollar bill across the table.

"So you two dinglenuts bet on whether I'd join you for coffee?"

"Don't take offense," Bill says as he folds the dollar carefully into his wallet. "We place bets on a variety of things to keep things interesting around here. Join us. We're glad you're here."

Dennis yips over to Filomena, "Make one more Irish coffee for Diana."

"Will do," she yaps back.

"Irish coffee? It's barely eight a.m. and we're already drinking?" I ask.

"Yes. Bill, Filomena, Estelle, and I enjoy a boozy specialty coffee on the mornings we review cold cases," Dennis explains.

Estelle slides out the chair next to her. "Sit here by me. You can help us."

I take a quick gander around the table. Bill looks snazzy today in a white turtleneck and a navy blue sport coat. Estelle is dressed identically to her sister in matching purple tracksuits that complement their glasses. I notice a theme with those two and their coordinated outfits. Dennis is wearing a suit jacket and slacks, as if he were at the office. Old habits die hard, I suppose.

When the coffees arrive, they are the most decadent morning drinks I've ever seen. The mugs are topped with whipped cream, green sprinkles, and a cherry.

"Goodness gracious," I exclaim in astonishment. "What exactly is in this?"

As she places the mugs in the center of the table, Filomena shares her recipe: "Baileys Irish Cream, Jameson Irish Whiskey, whipped cream, sprinkles, a cherry, and a dash of coffee." She smiles and winks. "To be honest, when it's my turn to craft them, it's more booze than brew. Enjoy!"

"This coffee recipe is Dennis's favorite," Estelle adds. "Diana, I hope you enjoy a tainted coffee now and again."

"I do like to indulge in a tickle of brandy in the evenings with my tea, but a boozy breakfast is a first for me," I admit. "However, I'm always open to trying new things. A warm, boozy drink on a chilly day like today seems lovely."

"It's colder than a witch's nipple out there," adds Bill.

One by one, everyone grabs a mug after quickly examining them. The sayings crack me up. Bill picks the mug that reads "I'm not a gynecologist, but I'll take a look." Dennis takes the one that reads "I may be wrong, but it's highly unlikely." Filomena's mug boasts, "I'd shank a bitch for you." Estelle's mug features a unicorn and says "Believe in yourself." Two mugs remain. One claims, "After this brew, I'm off for a poo," and the other states, "Retired, not my problem anymore." I choose this one. "This one fits me best," I say. "Who is the other mug for?"

"Carol, the nurse, will be here shortly," Filomena says.

"She might not care for the sentiment on her mug," I suggest.

"She's the one who buys these funny mugs at thrift stores and brings them here. She's a little twisted, like the rest of us," Bill says affectionately. "We love *her* —not her *needles*."

I fidget in my seat. My hip throbs from bending and stretching, opening boxes, and putting away whatever remains of my belongings, but after a few sips, I begin to feel better. My joints loosen, and I feel warm and tingly within minutes. I catch Dennis's attention and insist, "Tell me about these cold cases."

You can see the excitement on Dennis's face as his fat cheeks ruddy with anticipation. He pulls a manila file from his briefcase and places it in front of him. I can't help but notice that he's far too big for the chair. He must be so uncomfortable. As you age, the worst feelings are those of discomfort. This 275-plus-pound man has no business in this hazardous, tawdry chair. Bless this bareheaded monstrosity of a man for trying to feign comfort. I admire a man who endures a smidgen of pain for the greater good of the collective. I make a note to myself to have Rebecca buy a much larger, more comfortable chair.

Dennis begins. "First, let me explain. Last year, when I retired from the force, I had difficulty settling into retirement. I became restless, so I met with the police chief, who agreed to let me rummage through some cold case files to work on in my spare time."

"I absolutely love this! How can I help?" I feel a smile spread across my face.

"I appreciate your willingness to help, but I'll address that part later," he says quietly.

"Alright," I say.

"Here are the cold case facts: As of 2022, nearly three hundred forty thousand homicides remain unsolved in the United States, dating back to 1965. Florida accounts for six percent of the nationwide total, with just over twenty thousand cases."

"That's a lot of unsolved crimes." I listen carefully to every word with bated breath. This is so interesting. I am already thinking about calling Lola and telling her all about my new friends. I reel in my thoughts and continue to listen.

"Attorney General Ashley Moody established Florida's Cold Case Investigations Unit to assist local law enforcement agencies, particularly those with limited resources. The unit provides additional resources to selected unsolved cases. Not all cold cases are presumed homicides. In simplified terms, a cold case simply means it's unresolved. Cold cases may turn out to be accidental deaths or runaways. But, sadly, most cases end up closed within the murder category. Our small team here works on some of the most challenging ones."

"Challenging in what way?" I lean in, fully invested and intrigued, waiting for his reply.

Dennis lets out an exasperated sigh. "How can I answer this without you thinking we're looney tunes?" If his head were transparent, I could see the wheels turning.

He pauses just long enough for Filomena to chime in. "Please don't run off after I tell you this!"

I nod in agreement. "Go ahead, tell me."

"Promise me," she insists.

"Alright. Dagnabit. Just get on with it!" I groan and fidget in my chair.

"You might not like what you hear. Please don't run away." Estelle squeezes my hand.

Filomena blurts out, "I read tarot cards while my sister, Estelle, talks to dead people."

I try to keep my mouth from falling open, but I fail. I say nothing because I can't find the words. I'm shocked. No, more like bewildered. The only sound I make is my jaw cracking open. Everyone's eyes are fixed on me. I pull my hand away from Estelle's. "Oh," I finally manage, having no other idea how to respond.

Filomena jumps back in quickly, noticing my discomfort. "Bill is our tech guy, and Dennis is our night stalker."

I nearly jump out of my seat, startled by the dragging screech of the chair against the tile as Carol sits down next to Bill, looking like a ragamuffin. She's a short, portly woman. Her blouse is ruffled, her hair tangled, looking like it could use a good washing, and she's entirely out of breath.

"What did I miss?" she huffs.

"Why are you so breathless?" Filomena asks.

"I had to rush over from the clinic. I didn't want to be late. We're busy today with a stomach bug that's going around. Puke everywhere. It's nasty over there."

"How nasty is it?" Bill makes his eyebrows dance, egging her on with a challenge.

Carol rises to the challenge and swiftly retorts, "Nastier than a pastor's daughter's first year in college."

I nearly spit coffee out of my nostrils. I wipe my nose and try not to seem alarmed.

"Nice one," Bill says, and Dennis nods in agreement. The men lift their mugs to Carol, recognizing her clever remark.

"Carol, this is Diana. She's new here," Filomena says.

"Hi, Diana. I heard all about the kerfuffle caused by your arrival yesterday. A moving truck, a Bentley with a driver, and your redheaded sexpot assistant creating a stir and bossing people around the property."

"I'm sorry for all of that. Everyone was eager to help me settle in quickly. I apologize."

Bill perks up. "Tell me more about this sexpot assistant of yours."

"Back to business," Dennis insists. "Here we go." He rubs his bald head and opens the file. "Today's case involves a nine-year-old girl who went missing in 2001 while playing in the backyard. Her mom was finishing up dinner, and when she went to check on her, the girl had vanished. The police thoroughly investigated the family, neighbors, and friends but found nothing." Dennis distributes copies of the case file to each of us.

As I look around the table, each member of this group seems fully invested in finding this killer. I can feel my heart beating faster beneath my sweater. This is really exciting.

"My sister and I will see what we can come up with this evening. I'll observe what the cards reveal, and Estelle will uncover any messages that may come through from the other side. I'm sure we can expose something important," Filomena assures us. "Do you have anything that belonged to her?"

"Yes." Dennis retrieves a red sweater and a stuffed bunny from his briefcase and hands the items to Estelle.

Estelle's face lights up. "I really love a new case. It's so thrilling. I can't wait to hold a late-night chat with my deceased friends."

Bill checks the calendar on his phone. "I'm available all day tomorrow. I'll explore the dark web to see if I can find anything related to child abduction and trafficking in her area during that time period."

"Bill is the only one among us who really understands computers," Dennis explains. "Digital stuff. Things even cyber police units can't find."

Bill further explains, "A lot of what I do is in the grayer area on the black-and-white spectrum. Pink Floyd's *Dark Side of the Moon* would be a lyrical example."

"So you're a hacker?" I spit out.

"Please use your indoor voice and kind words in here," Bill teases.

Filomena places her hand over Bill's. "I worry about you sometimes. Are you sure you're ready for this? Kid cases and the dark web can lead to dark places."

"Does Dolly Parton sleep on her back?"

"I'll take that as a yes," Dennis responds with a nod.

"There's always some creep who thinks too much time has passed for them to get caught. Criminals love to brag, and their friends, even more so," Bill says reassuringly.

"Thank heavens someone here knows their way around the web," I say. "I'm not averse to technology myself, but it's not for me. It moves too quickly for someone my age to keep up. I once had an Insta—as the kids call it. You know, Instagram. I kept getting messages from people asking if I wanted to watch them . . . how shall I say this . . . um . . . play with their bag of groceries? So I don't engage online any longer. Nope. This is not for me! You keep your jar of nuts to *yourself*, and I'll keep my lady bits and flower garden to *myself*."

"You're missing out," Bill offers, winking his blue glass eye. "Groceries are expensive these days—nuts especially."

"I never get *those* scam messages. I only get emails about tolls that need to be paid from my imaginary car or bail to be paid to someone in Asia for an imaginary relative—only the boring scams," Estelle says with a huff.

"I understand criminals, finagling flimflam men, and your garden variety hooligans rather well," I brag. "I'm sure I can be of *some* use here."

Carol raises her hand as if she's in class.

"Yes," Dennis replies to her question.

"Um, I'm assuming that since this case is twenty-four years old, no pets are still alive." Carol's voice wavers, and she appears upset.

"Correct," says Dennis. "We might not need you on this case."

"Oh, phooey! I was hoping for something better than vomit to keep me occupied over the next few days."

Mr. Anderson, the resident cat, rubs against the table and Carol's leg before starting to meow beneath the table. Carol taps Bill's arm. "Your wallet fell. It's under the table."

Bill peeks under the table and responds, "Jumpin' juggernaut."

How on earth did she know that? I wonder, but before I can ask, she replies, "Mr. Anderson told me. Everything has a voice; you just have to listen."

Carol sucks down the remaining coffee in her mug. "I gotta go. Time to poo," she teases, holding up her mug to comply with its instructions. "Good luck with the case," she adds, then rushes off to the clinic.

"What *exactly* does Carol do?" I ask.

"In addition to being a nurse at our clinic, Carol possesses an uncanny ability to empathize with the animals left behind or those at the scene. She's somewhat of a pet whisperer."

"Fascinating," I murmur. It's the only word that comes to mind.

"I hope you don't see us as a bunch of crazy fools or believe we think we're muggles pretending to be wizards in an imagined world of Hogwarts. We have genuinely solved cold cases in the past year," Filomena explains.

"Seven cases, to be exact," Dennis clarifies.

"Go ahead and ask Dennis how many cases we've worked on," taunts Estelle.

"How many?" I play along.

"Seven." Dennis straightens up in his chair, proud of this accomplishment. "We have a perfect record."

"Wow, impressive. I know how I can help," I offer. "I know almost every politician in town, and given the undisclosed sum of money my family paid to distract them from the issues surrounding sugar harvesting, many owe me favors—big favors. I'm eager to help. I never wanted to retire anyway. I'm excited to make a difference in the world. It will feel good to work on the helpful side of humanity. Help is greater than harm."

Dennis twiddles the fingers of his right hand—the universal sign for give me cash.

Bill opens his wallet, unfolds the dollar bill, and slides it over to Dennis. "We're even for the day," Bill says, acknowledging his defeat. The two men glare at each other as if I'm not even there.

"Another bet? I'm not a toy." My cheeks flush, but I remain calm.

Estelle spurts out, "Diana, if a man treats you like a toy, be Annabelle."

Funny, that's one of my daughter's favorite horror movies. It brings a smile to my face, and suddenly I'm not annoyed any longer.

"I'm sorry, Diana. I didn't think a sophisticated lady like you would be interested in this kind of drudge work or willing to explore unsavory and unconventional ways our little group uncovers information. I was wrong, and I stand corrected. However, I'd love to hear more about your sugar secrets, sugar lady," Bill quips, strategically trying to change the subject.

"I'm sure you would. Most of the tales I have to tell will be disclosed through my memoirs one day, long after I'm dead. Too spicy for today's times." I spin my Tiffany bracelet. One, two, three times. I prefer odd numbers. Odd numbers are unique and special; they stand alone outside of the box, so to speak. I remind myself to breathe and not wallow in the thought of the bombshells I'll reveal once my memoir is published.

"I'm not sure there's anything that's too spicy for today's times," Filomena says, shaking her head. Estelle nods in agreement.

"I'll tell you this: My family has spent millions on election and reelection campaigns, surpassing the number of years I've been alive."

Suddenly I hear a moan, and I whip my head around to see a thin, haggard man wearing a Mets baseball cap sitting by the window. He's grasping his tallywacker as if it had just escaped from the zipper of his jeans, and he doesn't know how to wrangle it back into place.

"Ziggy, put your pissing stick away," Bill demands. "You took too many meds again. Carol warned you not to be too aggressive with the Ambien."

Ziggy stares at Bill vacantly. He begins to sway in his chair, gripping his escaped appendage for dear life.

"Those meds make you act strangely, Ziggy. Just one pill a day. Keep that in mind next time," Bill advises.

"So sorry," Ziggy slurs with a mouthful of oatmeal mush. "I need to pee."

"Don't mind Ziggy," Estelle whispers. "He's a sweet man. Harmless. I assure you, he won't remember this tomorrow."

Filomena says, "Yeah. Nice fella. The porch light's on, but no one's home, if you know what I mean."

Bill adds, "He hasn't got the sense God gave a goose—poor fella. His mind is slowly disintegrating into mush. He probably belongs in one of those hippie chic end-of-life places where they pick daisies by day, dance in the rain, and sing 'Kumbaya' by the campfire at night. I'll text Carol to retrieve him and get him back to bed."

"Back on track . . . let's get started . . ." Filomena leans in, placing her elbows on the table. "Tell us all the details about the day this little girl went missing."

Chapter Five

Mr. Anderson

If you think high school was hard, wait until you move into a fifty-five plus community. High school drama queens have nothing on the self-absorbed, well-to-do men and women who seem to have too much time on their hands. That's merely my perspective. Take it or leave it.

Sometimes it's important to get away from it all. On brisk, cool days like today, I enjoy walking through the gardens. The wind rustling through my whiskers makes me feel alive. Rats seek shelter from the cold, so there isn't much to chase today. At my age, I'm too slow to catch rats anyway.

On a typical day, you'd find Ziggy feeding peanuts to his two favorite squirrels. He named them Laverne and Shirley, although I'm pretty confident one of them is male. Today, since Ziggy retreated back to bed after breakfast (something about pulling out his privates in public), I'm strutting through the gardens alone.

The tranquility of the park and the sound of the babbling brook remind me of the mornings I spent with old man Monty before sunrise, watching the birds awaken, and the forest rustle back to life after its nighttime slumber. Monty understood the Earth's need for bees, birds, trees, and clean water. As beautiful as the park is, I can't help but feel lonely. I miss my friend; I miss Monty.

Joni Mitchell's "Big Yellow Taxi" plays in my mind, reminding me of those moments we shared together. Monty fought hard for this space to be built. He transformed the vacant lot at Ocean's Edge into a beautiful park beloved by all the residents. He refused to, in the words of Joni Mitchell, *pave paradise to put up a parking lot.* So what if we now have to share the parking space with the cemetery next door? It's all worth it in the end.

I make a promise to myself: I'll make sure the person responsible for killing Monty gets their just desserts. The bodies can only pile up so far before the perpetrator gets caught. I'm here to watch it all unfold with a little nudge from my direction.

What's that saying? Hell hath no fury like a feline scorned? Not exactly, but something like that.

Chapter Six

Diana
First Cold Case

Three days pass before we agree to meet and discuss our findings. Dennis's text from last night suggested that we write down any information we uncovered and place it in an envelope. I did my part, and I'm eager to disclose my revelations. I'm rushing around my townhouse like a madwoman getting ready when I remind myself to slow down. Where in God's gracious Earth am I going in such a rush? As I get older, I tell myself it's okay to take an extra beat or two, or I'll miss a beat or two. It's good advice. I should listen to myself more often.

This morning, I was so dizzy with excitement that I had to double back to my townhouse twice, forgetting first my phone and then my purse. On the last go-round, I catch a glimpse of myself in the hallway mirror. I look pretty foxy for a retiree, if I may say so myself. I have a little lower abdomen jelly roll that I call my "Lola roll." It's easy enough to hide. I'm proud of it. Lola was difficult to conceive, and my little roll is a reminder of the best part of me—

something only a mom can relate to. I was once an apple-eating size six, but I traded it all in for champagne, French toast, and good ol' southern fried chicken. Over the years, I've learned anyone can look fabulous. You don't need to be a size six. It's all about fit and fabric. I've got a dress designer on the payroll who's a genius at making a few extra pounds disappear as though they never existed. So I'll eat and be merry until the mirror or my designer says otherwise.

The country club is bustling with residents this morning. Saturday mornings draw everyone out to socialize. How do Saturdays differ from Tuesdays? I have no idea. Isn't every day the same when you're retired? I'll find out soon enough, I suppose.

When I arrive, Bill is busy at the coffee station, focused on crafting our morning boozy coffee. I catch a whiff of his cologne before he notices me walking toward him. Sauvage by Christian Dior reminds me of husband number four, causing my stomach to churn and growl in displeasure. That man was irritating. He would pull on my nightgown on the nights he wanted sex. My stomach growls louder in protest at the intruding memory.

"Mornin', sugar momma." Bill hands me a warm mug.

"Smells like chocolate," I say.

"This one is my specialty. My concoction includes coffee, a splash of vanilla vodka, a half shot of Godiva Chocolate Liqueur, and a dash of French vanilla creamer. It tastes like candy. I call it Velvet Bliss."

"Isn't that your drag queen name?" I tease.

He chuckles. "You've seen me perform?"

"Only on TikTok," I bluff.

"Enjoy it now. Who knows how long TikTok will be around before it's banned," he huffs.

"Government ruins all the fun," I huff back, shaking my head.

"The mugs are boring today," he apologizes. "Full house around here. All the good mugs are taken, so we're left with these stupid dancing Santas."

"That's fine. Who doesn't love Santa?"

"Um, the Grinch?" he taunts with a shrug.

I point out, "Even the Grinch came around in the end."

"Good point," he admits.

I help carry the three other mugs to a table by the window. Dennis arrives moments later, with Filomena and Estelle trailing behind.

"We have so much to report," cheers Estelle as she settles in.

"Velvet Bliss, my favorite." Filomena beams, reaching for her mug.

Before savoring his first sip of coffee, Dennis wastes no time opening his briefcase and pulls out a rendering of what the missing nine-year-old girl would look like today.

"You're not going to need that," Estelle says. "Put it away. It's too disturbing to see what she would have looked like at thirty-two. She's not with us anymore. Let's enjoy a little Velvet Bliss before we dive into all of this."

"So, Diana, how are you settling in?" Filomena asks, changing the subject.

"Very well," I say. I'm unsettled by Estelle's comment, but I can tell that she doesn't want to delve into her findings yet, so I go along with the subject change request and explain, "My assistant, Rebecca, and I have been working diligently to get the townhouse decorated. We installed shades and drapery, so I can sleep in or roam around freely in the nude if I choose to."

"Diana! You walk around all free willy? Thanks for the visual. Tell me more." Bill's expression indicates that he wishes for me to continue this conversation in another direction, but I resist.

"Well, I'm currently working on purchasing some new cozy living room furniture." I ask the twins, "What have you two been up to?'

Filomena's cheeks flush with excitement. "This week, we've played canasta and bunco and painted flamingos on canvas in the breezeway. Last night, we attended karaoke with Dancing Dapper Dan. Tonight is movie night, and you should join us. They're showing *Driving Miss Daisy* with Morgan Freeman and Jessica Tandy."

"Jeepers, do you two ever miss a social occasion?"

"No soiree happens around here without these two present," Bill points out.

Filomena and Estelle glance at each other and recite the tagline from the community brochure. " 'Never a dull moment where the land meets infinity. Discover the wonder at The Ocean's Edge,' " they say sarcastically in unison. They remind me of an Asian version of Lucy and Ethel, except that they dress identically. Today, matching black velvet tracksuits and black horn-rimmed eyeglasses.

Filomena adds, "The brain doesn't like to be bored. Keeping yourself busy staves off dementia."

Dennis, tapping his fingers on the table and looking irritated, urges, "Is now a good time to begin? Just let me know . . . I'll wait."

"Who pissed in your Cheerios today?" teases Bill.

"No one," Dennis answers. "I'm just a bit taken aback by what Estelle said about little nine-year-old Molly. Is she really dead?"

"Yes." Estelle opens her envelope. "I wrote down a few words that a visitor from the other side shared. I think the woman I was talking to was her grandmother. I can't be sure. She said the words 'ice cream and a red bracelet,' then told me to look in the garden. That's what I got. But I got an overwhelming feeling that she was no longer with us. I felt as though she is long buried, beneath us somewhere."

Filomena chimes in next, opening her envelope. "Once Estelle told me she may no longer be with us, I asked the cards where we could find her. Initially, I pulled two cards from my tarot deck. I pulled the Ace of Pentacles and the Ten of Cups. The Ace of Pentacles illustrates a garden with flowers. The Ten of Cups showcases a happy family with children dancing in the garden and a home in the distance. As a clarifier, I pulled the Magician card. I think she knew the man who took her and that he somehow entertained her or enamored her away from the yard in order to abduct her."

After hearing all of this, the tiny hairs along the back of my neck begin to tingle. I tap my foot under the table, biding my time, waiting for my turn to open my envelope.

"You look like you're about to jump out of your skin," says Estelle. "Are you feeling alright? I apologize if this is too much for you. Truly."

I feel itchy and anxious. "Yes, I'm peachy. No. It's not too much for me. I'm excited to report what I uncovered."

"Pray tell, sugar sister," says Filomena.

That reference makes me smile, and for a moment, I feel connected to these people, like we are doing something really special here. "Well," I begin, "I made a phone call to the retired sheriff in Martin County, where this took place. He gave me the phone number of a retired detective named Sampson, who coincidentally used to play poker with my father. He was happy to help."

I pull out an envelope containing three pages of copious notes and hand it over to Dennis. He opens the envelope as I continue. "He remembered this case as one of the few that went unsolved under his purview. He said he personally interviewed everyone —the parents, neighbors, friends, etc.—and came up with nothing. A few years back, he said he was having a drink at The Goose Pub in downtown Jensen Beach when a man sat beside him."

"The Goose Pub? The old Harper's? That place is iconic. It's the best one-star dive bar you'll ever enjoy! Cheap drinks, great old-time rock and roll from the jukebox, and the most entertaining unsavory characters in town with stories that'll keep you up at night."

"Shut up, Bill," demands Dennis.

Bill rolls his eyes.

"The Goose sounds delightful. Maybe we can go on a field trip one day. Until then, let me finish," I snap. "He said they got to chatting, and the man mentioned he used to own an ice cream truck. He said he sold it to a young man across the street because he was afraid to quit his job at the time. He bought the truck on a whim but never used it. He wanted to pursue a new career, but he had four kids then, and he was concerned he wouldn't be able to pay his mortgage. So he sold the ice cream truck. Anyway, that's when it hit Sampson, he said." I lean in and pause for effect.

"What hit him?" They all chime in at different times.

"The week or two that he conducted interviews on that street, this ice cream truck kept circling the block. He noted that it was strange because kids were not out of school yet."

"Jesus Christ on crutches! Ice cream, like Estelle said," Bill clarifies in astonishment.

"I inquired whether he had looked into this individual. He replied that he had. His name was Brandon Jeffrey."

"Was?" Dennis perks up.

"Yes. It seems he perished in a tragic car accident a few weeks after Molly disappeared," I explain.

"Did your detective friend find any interesting information about him that we can work with?" asks Dennis. "I didn't see anything about this ice cream man in the cold case file."

"He came from a large family, with two brothers and four sisters. His mother kicked him out at age seventeen, and he spent some time in the military. He then returned home to buy a house nearby and drove an ice cream truck to make a living. All of this information is printed for you. He has no prior offenses, and since he died shortly after the little girl went missing, he wasn't pursued further."

"I have a sneaking inclination that he was kicked out for messing with his sisters." Bill's cheeks flush in anger. "Nothing's worse than men who mess with little girls."

"Dennis, you might want to speak to his mom if she's still alive," Filomena suggests.

"There's no need for that. I have the ice cream man's address," I tell them.

"Share the address; I'll look up the history of the home, and now that we have a name, I'll see what I can uncover about him on the dark web," Bill offers. "I think we should visit his old house and see what we can discover."

"Field trip—yippee!" say both Filomena and Estelle.

"Will we need a warrant?" I ask. There is so much to learn about such things.

I can hear Dennis's excitement when he answers, "Maybe. Let's do a drive-by and observe how much we can recognize of the backyard from the sidewalk. We can take a glimpse to see if there's a garden or remnants of one."

"I'll call my driver," I insist.

"We can't all fit in the Bentley, can we?" asks Filomena.

"No, I'll ask my driver, Jeb, to bring the company SUV; it accommodates eight people."

Bill flashes a broad smile. "Let's blow this popsicle stand! Time to discover what the ice cream man has hidden in his secret garden."

Chapter Seven

Martha Stewart has many words of wisdom for us peasants. One of her most popular ones is "Learn something new every day," but my favorite is "You're never too old to reinvent yourself." 2025 is my year to vacate the old and embrace the new me.

I decided journaling may be a good way to release the black cloud hovering over my soul. I understand that writing down my innermost thoughts can trap disturbing events of the past in order to improve my well-being in the present, so I'll give it a go. Bad memories have edges like scabs on a wound. I'll release these memories on paper. I'll let them go, so to speak. I won't keep picking at these scabs. It's not healthy. They won't heal. I'll tell my stories. My body and soul will heal, and I will finally be at peace.

I'm no eloquent writer, although I've done my fair share of clanging the keyboard on my light-blue two-tone Royal Safari typewriter. Am I afraid that someday someone will read all about the atrocities I've committed? No. I welcome it.

No better time than the present to write about my first kill. You know what they say: You never forget your first!

Dear Diary. No. Scratch that.

Dear Reader,

You have no idea what you've stumbled upon. This story is a doozy. Hold on tight. It's a bumpy ride!

Sunday, January 6, 1963

I used to sleep with a nightlight so that darkness couldn't completely take over the night. For my birthday, my mother bought me a lighthouse to help keep my room illuminated and the night terrors at bay. I love that lighthouse, and to this day, it continues to keep me safe in the darkest of times.

My birthday party had all the markings and potential of a perfect day. All the local kids and every one of my best friends from school were in attendance. Presents were stacked up a mile high in the kitchen, and Mom and Dad seemed to be getting along swimmingly, for once.

My friends and I enjoyed Clarabell, the clown, and her magic tricks. However, I found it interesting that no one recognized that she was once our first-grade teacher. Few people look beyond the facade, especially when magic and cake are involved.

It wasn't long after the presents were opened that my father began to get irritated with my mother. This time, from what I could tell, she was spending a bit too much time chatting up our neighbor Jim, who was newly divorced from his wife. My father would suck in his spit through his teeth when he was angry. Disgusting. Nevertheless—a clue to stay away.

He yanked her hair and dragged her into the bedroom, losing a high-heeled shoe along the way. No one stepped in to defend her; instead, the neighbors took this altercation as a cue to collect their children and scurry home as quickly as possible. No one helped her!

Now it was just Clarabell and me left with my abusive dad and a screaming mom. I was angry—very angry. In this crucial moment, I learned a valuable life lesson: Fear clouds the mind, but anger sharpens it.

Clarabell—Miss Jackson, as we called her in school—ran to the kitchen and dialed 0 to contact the police. I seized the cake knife, rushed into the bedroom, and did what I had to do.

I was eight years old.

Chapter Eight

Diana
Finding Molly

When Jeb arrives at The Ocean's Edge in the company SUV, I can read the excitement on everyone's faces. Smiles all around. A thrilling buzz fills the air. A familiar exhilaration washes over me, as though I'm back in the boardroom.

"This is going to be fun," Estelle gushes.

"Wow, what a ride!" Filomena can barely contain her enthusiasm.

Jeb comes around to open the doors, and Bill assists.

"Big fella, you can sit up front," Jeb suggests. "More legroom up here."

"Jeb, this is Dennis," I say, proceeding with the introductions and morning pleasantries as we all settle into the cozy leather seats of the Lincoln Navigator.

Lincoln is an iconic American company that was owned by Henry Leland, a longtime friend of my grandfather's. Now the company is owned by Ford Motors. I hear my grandfather's voice in my head: We live in America. Honor that. Buy American. We create just as many beautiful things as our foreign friends, but only *American goods* put food on *American tables*. Our cars are the finest.

Sometimes I wish he were still around. He had so much wisdom and could teach this new generation a thing or two about grit, loyalty, and determination.

"Alright, boss, where are we headed?" Jeb asks, glancing at me in the rearview mirror while adjusting the dial of the car's satellite radio. He switches the station to seventies rock. Led Zeppelin greets us with "Stairway to Heaven," and the irony here doesn't escape me as we begin our search for Molly.

Dennis connects his phone to the car's navigation system. "All set," he says, adjusting his seat for comfort. Off we go.

We immediately feel disappointed when we arrive at the ice cream man's house.

Bill speaks first. "This is not what I expected. Google Earth needs to update this street."

"I don't feel uneasy at all in this place," Estelle says, rubbing her fingers across Molly's sweater, which is nestled on her lap.

The house is dilapidated in multiple ways, with the roof missing and only two walls remaining standing.

"I bet this house was struck by a tornado during Hurricane Milton last October," Dennis says.

The backyard is small and littered with fallen trees.

"This isn't the spot," Estelle grumbles in disappointment.

"Now what?" asks Filomena with an exasperated sigh.

"Let's go to Molly's house," suggests Bill. "After researching the ice cream man and finding very little about him online, I looked deeper into Molly's father, and he seems like a real louse. That's being kind, with respect to the ladies."

"What do you mean? I checked the file and the recent police records; he has no prior arrests." Dennis fumbles through the file to reaffirm his statement.

Bill opens the notes app on his phone. "Her dad associates with a group of questionable characters. I identified a few of his friends from his Facebook photos linked to a biker gang in Georgia. Not that there's anything immediately wrong with bikers; the guys who frequent Lure's Bar & Grill in Jensen Beach are friendly enough. However, this biker gang in Georgia is mired in trouble—drugs, illegal guns, assault."

"So what are you saying exactly?" I ask.

"I'm not sure. Let's drive by Molly's and check," he suggests, looking at Dennis for approval. Dennis tells the car to navigate to her house, which is only two blocks away.

As soon as we pull up to her home, Estelle yelps. "This is it."

The hairs on the back of my neck and arms tingle. Spooky.

We all tumble out of the car onto the sidewalk. The house, although spared by the tornado from Hurricane Milton, sits abandoned with a For Sale sign swaying in the wind. The sign features a provocative photo of a beautiful woman and the tagline "Home is Where You'll Find Me." It's a creepy sign, considering the circumstances. We must have all been thinking the same thing, because we stare at each other in eerie stillness. Even Bill has no witty response.

Dennis leads us down the sidewalk toward the backyard gate. "It's locked." He yanks on the lock to confirm his initial assessment.

"I'm here for you, dude." Bill pulls what looks like a bobby pin from his bun and jams it into the lock, which opens easily. Upon closer inspection, I see that it's a lockpick—a thin piece of metal that hooks slightly at the tip and, I imagine, could open a lock just as effectively as it can clean plaque from your teeth.

"Where did you get that?"

"From my bun. You *watched* me pull it out," Bill says with a sarcastic smirk.

"I mean, ugh, never mind. What other doohickeys do you have hiding in that rat's nest?"

"That's for me to know and you to wonder." Bill pats his head, then adds, "Dinner, a few drinks, and if and only if you treat me with a bit of respect, *maybe* you'll find out." He raises his eyebrows several times, making them dance.

What a strange man. I poke at his hair for fun to see if anything else will slip out.

"Hey, respect for my man do." Bill pats his bun gently.

"Okay, lovers, enough canoodling between you two." Dennis jokes. My stomach churns, and I can taste the bile rise. Lovers? Never. Not funny.

What we discover next is deeply unsettling. While the house itself could use some TLC, the yard is immaculate. It's teeming with vibrant pink and red pentas, orange birds of paradise, and purple Mexican heather, all centered around a large southern magnolia tree. In the right corner of the yard, a teak bench is nestled among large shrubs adorned with purple flowers.

"Oh shit," I say. "I mean, oh, sugar schnitzel," I correct myself.

"We're not home . . . you can swear in public," Bill reminds me.

"Oh, right." I shrug. It's funny how once you tell yourself not to do something, like swearing, it becomes difficult to revert back. The mind is strange that way.

"Do you know what those shrubs are called?" I continue my thoughts as Bill unlatches the gate and we trespass onto the property.

"It's muhly grass, a native saw grass, but it's also known as Miss Molly butterfly bush."

Faces widen in shock, jaws drop, and Estelle walks over to the bench to take a seat. "She's here."

"I'll call it in. I'll get a crew out here to dig."

"Can you? On what grounds?" I ask. "The name of a bush and a so-called feeling from Estelle? No offense, Estelle. I shouldn't have said that. I didn't mean to be dismissive." Ugh, I remind myself not to be so harsh. Use kinder words, Diana. You're retired —be nice to people, I tell myself.

"No offense taken," she responds, unbothered by my remark. She's so sweet.

"Hey, what's that under the bench?" asks Bill.

"I don't see anything." Filomena walks closer to the bench.

"I'm half blind and I can see something red underneath the bench," Bill says. Bill and Filomena both crouch down to scrutinize the object further.

"Don't touch that," Dennis demands. He retrieves a clear plastic bag from his jacket pocket and tweezers from another. He picks up the red object and places it in the bag.

"What is it?" I ask first.

Dennis holds the bag up to the sunlight. "A red bracelet. It's engraved *Molly*." Dennis's smile stretches from ear to ear. He's smiling like a possum. I get a creepy-crawly sensation along the back of my neck.

Estelle embraces her sister. "It's just as Filomena mentioned . . . a garden, a red bracelet."

It's impressive how Filomena interpreted both a garden and a red bracelet from her cards. We are experiencing exactly what she predicted. This moment feels both right and wrong. I often have these conflicting feelings in the boardroom when a deal seems too good to be true. I've learned to trust my gut; it's smarter than my emotions. "It seems careless to leave this evidence behind." I state the obvious.

Filomena suggests, "I bet that after all these years, assuming there's no real risk of getting caught, this was left behind intentionally as a loving gesture. Before moving out of the house, someone placed the bracelet, much like how people leave flowers and teddy bears at a grave."

"Let's go," Dennis insists. "I need to do some schmoozing at the station to get this ball rolling."

We drop Dennis off at the police station, and Jeb takes the rest of us to Chris' Martini Bar for a well-deserved drink. Espresso martinis to celebrate. We're going to need one, two, or perhaps a few to unwind.

"Three cheers to the hope that we find Molly."

Chapter Nine

Diana
A Call from Lola

I'm sitting on my new couch, watching episode four of the new season of *Dexter: Original Sin* when my cell phone rings.

"Hello, Mom."

"Oh, hello, Lola." I pause my show to give my daughter my full attention. We haven't spoken since I moved in. We typically talk a few days a week, despite all the noise and chaos surrounding my departure.

"How are you getting along with the OAPs?"

"OAPs?"

"You know, Mom . . . get with it . . . the old ass people?" She jokes. "Are you living your best pajama life? Working on your professional napper status?"

"It's funny. Laugh now, but one day you'll find yourself here."

"I hope so. God willing. That's if the company doesn't lead me to an early grave." She snickers. "I don't want to talk about work. How are you getting along? Making friends? Fun activities? Cute guys?"

"Yes to friends. I haven't attended any activities yet. There aren't many cute guys, but I haven't fully explored campus. I'll need more time to get acquainted with the fellas."

"The last thing you need in your life right now is a new man. Enjoy being single for a while, work on yourself, and please, no more husbands, Mom."

"Of course. No more husbands. Agreed."

"Dating could be enjoyable, though," she suggests.

"Dating after seventy is like trying to find the least damaged thing in a thrift store that doesn't smell."

Lola giggles like she's eight years old, and I'm brought back to the days when making her laugh was the highlight of my day. Her giggles are pure joy to me.

"I read that joke on a Facebook meme. You know what Facebook is, right? Social media for OAPs?"

"Yes, Mom, I'm aware. Don't be snarky, and . . . don't give up on yourself or dating just yet. One day you'll find a man who will appreciate your dark humor." I can hear the smile in her voice.

"I will try, my dear, but dating is merely a collection of lies and intolerable compromises. I may be too old for that. Perhaps a friend with benefits is what I need these days."

"Benefits . . . hmm. Just be nice, Mom. You catch more flies with sugar—"

I cut her off. "It works both ways. Men need to be nice to me first. And who's trying to catch flies anyway? What a stupid expression."

"How is Jeb?" she asks. "Are you keeping him busy? He must be bored out of his mind."

"Jeb has been driving me around town, and we discovered a trendy little coffee shop called The Googan. They serve this incredible Shark Bite energy drink that's to die for! It's perfect for a midday pick-me-up. We'll have to go when you visit. How is Lydia?"

"Fabulous. She's doing well in school. She's been asking about you. I think we'll visit over spring break. Unless, of course, by then you've found a new gentleman friend to tussle around with, and you're too preoccupied for us."

"I'm never too busy for my favorite heiress and her little sugar princess."

"Funny, Mom. You aren't mad at me, are you? I detect a hint of sarcasm in your voice."

"Please stop asking me that. It's been months. You ask me that every time we speak. No. I'm not mad at all. I'm proud of you. It was the best beheading a woman could ask for."

"There you go again with your snide, sarcastic comments. I can never tell if you're trying to be funny or if you're still bitter about the whole situation."

"Of course I feel a bit bitter. But you were right. It was time for me to leave. Honestly, retirement is the best thing that has happened to me in quite a while. I'm having a great time and can't wait for you to visit so I can tell you all about it."

"Thank you, Mom. I love you."

"I know you do. Let me share what I've been doing. It's quite exciting."

"Fantastic. Go on."

"Well, I helped solve a cold case," I tell her proudly. Then I hear the phone clamor to the floor with a thud. There's a moment of silence before Lola returns.

"Lydia, Mommy is talking. Hush, sweetie. I'm talking to Grandma . . . sorry, what now?"

"Oh, nothing, my dear. Take care of my little princess. I look forward to seeing you soon. Talk then."

Chapter Ten

Diana
Molly Recap

The whole gang waits for me as I enter, rolling in a genuine leather executive swivel chair with large armrests for comfort. Dennis's face lights up like a child on Christmas Day.

"This is for you, my friend," I tell him. "You look so darn uncomfortable in these plastic Walmart stackable folding chairs. It should be a damn near crime for anyone on the flip side of a half-dollar to set their rusty-dusties in these. Now you can sit in comfort. We just need to make sure it's reserved only for you and none of your fellow resident fartbags."

"Good luck with that," Bill mumbles, rubbing his knee, his face wincing in pain.

"What's the matter with your knee?" I ask.

"It's going to rain today. My knee acts up whenever the weather becomes humid."

"The same thing happens to my elbow," Filomena adds.

"Must be an old age thing," Carol hisses as she pulls out a chair to sit at the table. "Nice chair, Dennis. A gift from the heiress?" Carol smiles at me. "Tell me all about the case."

"First things first. Coffee. No discussions before coffee." Dennis sways in his new chair, awaiting his liquid breakfast. "Thank you, Diana. I love the chair—very thoughtful. It might be the nicest thing anyone has done for me in quite a long time."

"That's sweet," I say, holding his gaze. His eyes well up, but he holds back his tears, and I can see he meant what he said. My heart melts a little, and I feel exposed. I want to say I haven't done anything nice for anyone in quite some time, and I love this too. But I know if I say that, we both might cry—and we're too old for that nonsense.

Estelle returns with Italian coffee just in time, and Bill helps carry it to the table. "You will love these," she boasts. "Frangelico, coffee, Italian sweet creamer, and a dollop of whipped cream. They're delightful."

Bill places both Sweet'N Low and raw sugar on the table. "I didn't know if anyone would want to add sugar to their coffee." Bill's eyes meet mine for approval.

"Don't ask me." I shake my head. "One will give you diabetes; the other will give you cancer. Pick your poison and enjoy your coffee."

Today's mugs all have bee themes. One says Bee Kind, another says Bee Mine, the third says Honey Bee, the fourth says Queen Bee, the fifth says Bee Happy, and the last says Let it Bee. I grab the Queen Bee mug.

"Carol, what's with the bee mugs? Are these new?" asks Filomena.

"No, I didn't buy these. Before Monty died, he purchased a bee colony for the gardens. It was delivered yesterday, along with the mugs."

"Bees?" Dennis rubs his head.

"Apparently, they're honey bees. The bees were among the last purchases Monty made before he passed. They're harmless and essential for the planet's health," Carol explains.

"I can attest to that. We had an abundance on the sugar farm. I grew up surrounded by bees. My grandfather used to say that if humans possessed the work ethic and loyalty of bees, the world would have no problems."

"Hear, hear!" Bill raises his coffee mug, and we all follow suit. We lift, clink, sip, and enjoy our first taste.

"Alright. Let's get down to business," Dennis says, pushing forward. "I'm pleased to report that we have successfully closed our cold case file."

A flurry of questions erupts from everyone across the table.

"You found Molly?"

"That was quick."

"Was she buried in the yard?"

"Did her father kill her?"

"I'll explain." Dennis lets out a deep sigh and takes a large sip of coffee. "I submitted a request to dig up the yard, and while I was waiting for the paperwork to be approved, I drove to visit her dad in Georgia."

"Long drive," Estelle replies.

"Yes, sure was. As soon as I stepped through the door, he asked, 'You found her?' I remained silent. Then he walked to the kitchen, grabbed two Heinekens, sat down across from me at the kitchen table, and explained everything."

Dennis pauses for a moment, rubs his bald head, and sips his coffee, seeking to build anticipation for the big reveal.

"Well, then what?" Carol asks. "Tell us. I need to get back to the clinic. I haven't got all day!"

"How did he kill her?" asks Bill.

"He didn't." Dennis retrieves a family photo and places it in the center of the table.

The family is posed nicely in front of their home on a summer day. The father wears shorts and a short-sleeved shirt, while the mother and daughter are dressed in sundresses. They look like a perfectly happy family.

Dennis points to the mother. "The father told me that his wife and daughter were arguing. His daughter talked back to her mother, and the mother slapped her. The daughter fell and hit her head against the kitchen table. She died instantly. Lights out. The mother didn't call the police because she had been drinking at the time."

"Drinking?" Estelle and Filomena say in unison.

"She was undergoing chemotherapy for cancer, and the pain was reportedly unbearable. As a result, she turned to alcohol and pills. She was not in a condition to talk with the police—apparently not in her right mind at the time."

"Then what happened?" Carol scratches her unwashed hair. Her shirt is still stained from the last time I saw her. This woman either works very hard for long hours or neglects her self-care.

"The father took Molly to his brother's farmhouse, where he laid her to rest. A few years later, his wife passed away. He returned Molly home before moving away.”

“Sounds messy,” Bill says.

“The mother? I didn’t anticipate that one,” I say.

“Me neither,” Dennis says. “I didn’t even consider that the mother would have anything to do with it. She looked so sad and seemed so frail, fragile. I was way off base.”

Estelle asks, “So the ice cream man had nothing to do with this story? Why then was he circling the block at the time?”

“Maybe he was curious, suspicious, or maybe he was a pervert, who knows? He died too soon to get any real answers from him. Nevertheless, we solved our case,” Dennis boasts. “Every clue guided us toward the right destination. That’s how a police investigation operates, and ours was successful,” he adds with pride.

A roar of thunder, followed by flickers of light, and then rain—lots of it—pounds against the floor-to-ceiling windows surrounding us.

Bill points toward the window with an “I told you so” look on his face as he rubs his knee, while Filomena smiles and rubs her elbow.

Bill says, using a radio broadcaster’s voice, “Diana, welcome to The Ocean’s Edge! We hope you are enjoying your new friends who solve crimes and forecast the weather."

Another loud roar of thunder blasts, and we all share a good laugh. It feels refreshing to laugh again. I'm enjoying myself and my new friends. It's been a long time since I've truly allowed myself to have a good time. I feel the smile on my face grow deeper.

"One more question," Estelle says. "Did they arrest him?"

Dennis swivels in his new chair, making three complete circles like a child at the counter of an old-time soda shop. "I don't know. I'm retired. It's no longer my purview or my job to make those decisions. But, as of now, we are eight for eight in solving cold cases, so cheers to us!"

"Cheers to us!"

Chapter Eleven

Theo

There are some really strange characters around here. I had lunch today with a fella who claims he talks to Elvis in the garden on Tuesdays. Somehow or another, Elvis manages to find time to chat among the azaleas for Tuesday morning pleasantries and blueberry scones. From what I've been told, Elvis is a big fan of country line dancing and will be attending Saturday evening's Rednecks and Renegades party at the country club.

In these moments, I almost feel normal—just another resident enjoying a beautiful morning in the park, conversing with another resident about his imaginary friend.

Back at home, I remind myself that my existence in this world serves a purpose. My mind is sharp (unlike the strange resident today chatting with Elvis). My hands are agile, and I'm still able to purge the Treasure Coast of some truly terrible people. Life is short, getting shorter every day, and I've got work to do.

I fill a twelve-ounce glass with milk, then refill it after taking a few sips. I also pack a bowl with eight Oreo cookies, my favorite childhood treat. My mom often sent me to my room with milk and Oreos before my dad came home, trying to protect me from him. Looking back on that today, it's funny. In the end, that was obviously unnecessary.

I open my journal and begin my second entry.

Dear Reader,

Saturday, March 9, 1974

Beer, booze, girls, beautiful weather, and a pool provide all the perfect ingredients for a college fraternity party. With the finest sorority on campus, Delta Zeta, as guests for the evening, the night was bound to be a blast. Guests arrived around noon, and by 6 p.m. nearly everyone was drunk and stumbling out of the pool. It didn't take long for someone to notice a girl motionless at the bottom of the deep end. I was the one who jumped in to pull her out and perform mouth-to-mouth resuscitation. No luck. I was also the one who spoke with the police when they arrived. I was the one who witnessed exactly what happened.

This boy, whose name I won't reveal because he was the son of a state senator, was becoming a little too friendly with a particular sorority girl. She had no interest in him. It appeared that there was more to their relationship, as though this was not his first encounter with her. Despite her lack of interest, he continued to pester her. He pulled her aside when everyone was exiting the pool to devour hot dogs from the grill. Suddenly he got angry, snapped her neck, and threw her toward the deep end.

This was no accident. I saw him exit through the back gate. I didn't inform the police of that. I waited for him to return that evening. Once everyone was passed out and the chances of getting caught were minimal, I sneaked into his room and did what needed to be done.

Chapter Twelve

Mr. Anderson

Today, as I prance through the garden, I notice Carol and Tom sitting on the bench. I see them together often these days. I wonder what they're conspiring about. She's wearing soft, velvety leggings. Don't touch them, I tell myself. Be inconspicuous. No one has seen me yet. Get close and find out what they're talking about. But I have to touch those leggings; they look so soft. I can't resist. I rub against her leg. It just happens by reflex, without my permission. Cozy. So soft. I purr, sit, and look up at them. They stop talking. Ugh. Forget I'm here. I'm a spy. I've been terrible at my job lately. Stupid leggings distracted me!

"Hello, Mr. Anderson. How are you today? Did you chase any birds this morning?" Carol asks.

I lick my lips and look away. Sometimes she talks to me as if I'm a child. Tom doesn't acknowledge me at all; he hates cats. I feel invisible around him, and that's a good thing.

I don't know much about Tom, but I don't like him. I don't have a reason yet, but I'll find one. I heard him

say he served in one of those wars. I don't know
which one. Korea? Vietnam? The hats all look the
same. He talks too much and shares unnecessary
details about topics that nobody cares about. He's too
chatty. If you ask me, people who talk incessantly
have something to hide.

Chapter Thirteen

Diana
Another Cold Case

Rebecca's choice of venetian blackout blinds in my bedroom works so well that I've been waking up after 8 a.m. lately.

Today I stare at the digital clock on my nightstand in a panic. It's 8:07 a.m., and I have to remind myself that I'm retired. Why am I so upset that I slept in an extra hour or two? I deserve a bit of rest after a lifetime of ruthless deception, misdirection, and swindling as a sugar hustler. But, as they say, old habits die hard.

My grandfather used to say that to be successful, you need to rise even earlier than the worm. I was trained from an early age to be ruthless, to win at all costs. I was never taught how to enjoy success once I achieved it. Waking up after 8 a.m. harbors a dreadful feeling of weakness, as if I'm unworthy—a quitter. My predecessors worked until God struck them dead. Retirement is for pussies, my grandfather would say. Sorry, Pops, I gave it my all. This chapter in my life is entirely new to me, but I'm determined to make the best of it.

My phone dings with a group text message: *Meet in the courtyard at 9 a.m. New case. [File emoji]*

I roll out of bed, shower, get dressed, and rush over in record time. I'm the last to arrive. Carol, Filomena, Estelle, Bill, and Dennis wait patiently for me.

"You look chipper today. Did you get laid last night?" Bill asks with a stupid smirk on his face.

"I'm taking a break from men these days," I reply flatly. "The last thing I need is a new man in my life right now."

"Too bad. I'm great in bed, you know. Right, Estelle?" Bill nudges Estelle with his elbow, seeking endorsement.

"What?" Estelle's face turns two distinctly different shades of red. "How would *I* know that? *I've* never slept with you!" she huffs.

"Well, whose fault is that?" Bill shrugs.

That makes everyone laugh, just as a small passenger minibus pulls up to the entrance to pick us up.

I glare at Dennis. "I could have gotten the SUV. You should have told me."

"The cold case crimes unit provides it for us. We may not get paid in dollars, but we do have some resources we can take advantage of when they're offered," Dennis explains, rubbing his bald head. I've noticed he does this when he's nervous or put on the spot.

"Sure," I acknowledge.

"Also, I got into a bit of trouble regarding your SUV because Jeb is not a vetted team member—background checks and all that. Anyway, this will suffice for today's work."

"For heaven's sake! Here's the deal: I'll send over Jeb's background file, and you can get him approved, because it smells like wet socks and beef jerky in here," I declare after climbing the three steps onto the minibus.

"Right on, you have a good sniffer; that's exactly what it smells like," Bill agrees, climbing the steps behind me.

The driver snatches two empty jerky wrappers from the cup holder and stashes them in the front pocket of his jeans. "I'll stop by a CVS and pick up some Febreze air freshener later today. Sorry, folks."

"So what's this case about?" Filomena asks once we're all seated.

"You'll see when we get there," Bill taunts.

"I hate surprises," says Carol.

"That's rich coming from the person who shows up unexpectedly to jab us with toxic chemicals every few months," says Bill.

"It's for your own protection, continued health, and well-being," Carol groans. "Suck it, Bill."

"You know I will." Bill licks his lips.

"That's enough, kids." Dennis glares at Bill. "What's gotten into you today? No more caffeine for you."

"How long of a drive is it?" I ask, ignoring the queasy pang in my stomach while quietly trying to endure the rancid stench of this bus.

"Ten more minutes or so, I suppose," Dennis guesses. "Let's play a game to kill time."

"I love your games." Estelle grins from ear to ear. "Which game?"

"Name that serial killer," he says.

"For the love of Christ, really? Serial killers?" I protest.

"We'll play," Filomena and Estelle say in unison.

Those two always finish each other's sentences or speak in unison—twins are fascinating.

"I'll begin with something simple. The 1981 novel *The Red Dragon* eventually evolved into a series of films featuring actor Anthony Hopkins."

"Um, *Silence of the Lambs* . . . ah, Hannibal Lecter!" Estelle shouts, clapping her hands.

"Right," Dennis says.

"I loved that movie." Filomena congratulates her sister for getting the answer right with a fist bump. How cute!

"Can I go next?" asks Estelle.

"Sure." Dennis nods.

"Michael C. Hall plays a serial killer on Showtime who targets other serial killers. What is his character's name on TV?"

"Dexter," we all answer.

"That was easy," Carol says. "The last season, *Resurrection*, is being filmed as we speak."

"I've got another one," Dennis says. "Which serial killer was caught decades later for his crimes in California after genetic testing of his relatives?"

"The Golden State Killer," Bill answers.

"Yes." Dennis yells to the driver, "Turn here." Then he continues. "The Golden State Killer was a monumental case. It broke open cold cases worldwide through the use of DNA testing and genetic databases."

"This is fun." Estelle is giddy with delight.

"Y'all are sick . . . but I have one. Which Florida serial killer was executed in an electric chair known as Old Sparky?"

"Hmm," "I don't know," and "Shoot, who is it?" are the responses.

"Ted Bundy," I say proudly.

"How did you know that?" asks Bill.

"Ted Bundy killed girls years earlier in my daughter's sorority, so I heard a lot about him when she was rushing Chi Omega at Florida State."

Bill admits, "Don't tell anyone, but I hacked into the Florida State Prison once. I didn't read anything all that interesting, but I did learn that death row inmates only get a stipend of forty dollars that can be spent on their last meal. That meal also has to be purchased locally, within a five-to-ten-mile radius. So no Joe's stone crabs, or a tomahawk steak from Capital Grille. You'll most likely end up with a fancy Italian dinner and a McDonald's milkshake. The milkshake, however, is the most requested last meal beverage from what I've read."

"So interesting," I say as the minibus slows down to pass over a series of speed humps along the road.

"Okay, we're here." Dennis stands up from his seat to discuss parking details with the driver. "Please pick us up here in one hour," he informs him.

"Where are we?" I ask, wondering why the question slipped from my lips. It's clear where we are; the tombstones, oak trees, and eerie driveway reveal it.

"Graveyard," Dennis says, pointing out the obvious. "All Saints' Cemetery."

Once we scramble out of the rancid-smelling minibus, a professional couple in business suits is patiently waiting for our arrival with their dog on a leash.

Dennis shakes both their hands and then introduces the couple to us. "Everyone, meet Mr. and Mrs. Garrison. They are real estate moguls here on the Treasure Coast and own all the undeveloped land on South Hutchinson Island."

"Well, not *all*," Mrs. Garrison corrects him, "but a fairly substantial swath."

At first glance, you could tell Mrs. Garrison was once beautiful, but time and poor choices have taken their toll. Cigarettes and alcohol would be my guess by the deep, tiny wrinkles around her mouth and long, splintered broken capillaries on her ruddy cheeks and nose.

Mr. Garrison can only be described as a broken-down man who has seen better days. His face is worn and sullen, and he looks defeated before we even begin.

Dennis pulls a small notepad and a pencil from his pants pocket. The notes app on his phone would likely work just as well, if not better, but old-school detective skills die hard, I presume. "I'll let Mrs. Garrison explain why we are here today."

"For the record," she begins, "I think this is a terrible idea." She shakes her head and glances at her husband dismissively. "My husband is fascinated by Tyler Henry, that scrawny, overly emotional celebrity influencer who actually believes he can talk to dead people." Mrs. Garrison rolls her eyes. "So my husband, with his magical thinking, believes your little group of witches and wizards can solve the case of his missing daughter, my stepdaughter, Vanessa." She takes a deep breath and continues. "What you all do is poppycock, if you ask me, but have at it if you must!"

I take offense at her slurs. Who does this bitc— sorry, shrew, I correct myself mid-thought—think she is? Acting all-powerful in her cheap, poorly fitting suit and terrible blue hair dye job. Maybe she should find a salon with a professional stylist who uses toner! I scream out loud in my head. I'm not a bad feminist, I tell myself. I'm all for strong women. But *this* lady?

This lady comes off dastardly, like the other half of her hair should be dyed jet black, and she ought to be wearing a coat made from Dalmatian fur.

Anyway, she seems like a woman who initially appears well put together, but look deeper and you'll notice that she clearly does not come from money or have any real taste for style. She owns half the island and wears shoes from Nine West. Hogwash! And I know a fake Versace handbag when I see one. My guess is she's over-leveraged and her checkbook barely squeaks by with positive integers at the end of every month.

"Can I take your dog for a walk?" asks Carol. "What is his name?"

"Sure. His name is Amos," Mr. Garrison says as he hands Carol a T-shirt that belongs to his daughter. "My daughter Vanessa was sixteen when she disappeared. This was the last place she was seen."

"What was she doing here?" Dennis asks him, though I suspect he already knows the answer.

"She was visiting her sister's grave." Mr. Garrison wipes a tear from his cheek and hands the leash to Carol.

Carol walks up the hill with the T-shirt in hand and the dog in tow.

"Her grave is up ahead, in the seventh row on the right-hand side, four tombstones in," Mr. Garrison yells out as Carol and the dog walk off.

"I'm going to wait in the car." Mrs. Garrison's dark eyes shoot daggers at us, a wicked smile painted on her face. Then she storms off without a "thank you for helping" or a "goodbye."

Rage simmers within me like molten lava. I've known this woman for just a few minutes, yet I already hate her.

"How long ago did she disappear?" asks Estelle, wiping the excess moisture from the morning humidity off her eyeglasses.

"One year ago," Mr. Garrison answers.

"This is barely a cold case," Bill mumbles for only Dennis and me to hear.

I see Carol and Amos at the tombstone. She offers the dog a treat. He sniffs the shirt, and they both sit down at the gravesite. The dog seems more interested in sniffing Carol's scrubs than Vanessa's shirt.

"Are you sure this will be helpful, Dennis?" Mr. Garrison asks, appearing calmer now that his wife has left his side. "It's been so long. The police and private investigators have all tried to help." Mr. Garrison begins to cry. "I'm sorry. I'm just really frustrated."

Dennis consoles him. "I know, sir. We'll do what we can."

"Cold case my ass," I murmur quietly to Bill. "Are we certain this is *official* police business?"

Bill leans in and whispers, "It's a small town, Diana. I'm sure you, of all people, understand how family, business, and police work can intermingle."

"Of course I do," I say.

Bill says quietly, "It doesn't seem to me that he knows these people. Maybe the police chief? Or maybe this is a special favor from the mayor? No idea. But I'm sure he'll tell us. Dennis is not one for secrets."

Filomena strolls over the hill and sits beneath an ancient oak tree with her tarot cards.

Estelle walks past the mausoleum situated by the magnolia trees and takes a seat on a bench.

While Carol, Estelle, and Filomena are busy with their own tasks, Dennis is bombarding Mr. Garrison with questions about the night she disappeared, cross-referencing the information he finds in the file. Bill and I don't have much to do yet, so we walk across the street to the gas station for a Mountain Dew.

"You like Mountain Dew too?" Bill asks, surprised.

"Oh, honey, I'm a multigenerational Florida girl. Mountain Dew runs in my blood," I admit.

"Me too. I'm from the part of Florida where you can buy smoked mullet, boiled peanuts, fried alligator, and pickled pig tongue at the side of the road. I've been drinking Mountain Dew long before I found out it rots your teeth and brain cells. Now I drink it because I've already got one foot in the grave, and all that rot is well on its way, with or without Mountain Dew."

When we get in line with our drinks at the gas station counter to pay, a very elderly woman in front of us is hunched over the counter, rifling through her Coach purse for her checkbook.

"Sufferin' Jesus," I mutter so only Bill can hear me. "Who pays with a checkbook in this century? You may as well be trading with gold coins."

This makes Bill smile and he adds, "Yeah, she's pretty old. I wouldn't accept an apple from that lady. I wasn't aware we humans are allowed to live that long."

I play along and egg him on. "Well, how old is she?"

He's quick to respond. "I've seen younger faces on currency."

The old woman's hearing is still pretty sharp, because she whips her head around at my laughter and stares me down. Now I'm afraid she's hexed me for all eternity.

Bill and I slump down on a bench riddled with gum to enjoy our sodas. Nothing says bored teenagers like sticky pink patches of goo.

"What do you think of that Garrison woman?" Bill asks.

"Hate her all the way down into my varicose veins. I don't trust her," I admit, cracking open the plastic cap of my soda.

"Me neither. Can I ask you a personal question?" Bill takes a swig of Mountain Dew.

"Only if I can ask one back." I look at my watch. "A quick one."

"How is it that *you* took over your grandfather's company and not your father?"

"Good question. No one ever asks me that. My grandfather was a strong believer in following one dictator at a time. He served as the president and CEO. He sent both his sons to law school to study corporate law. He wanted to ensure that no government entity could take him down. My dad, uncle, and their team of lawyers were brilliant and powerful. It was a smart decision. He had too big of an ego to leave the company to one of his sons. I've worked for the company since college, handling every task—in the field, in secretarial work, in the warehouse, at the refinery, and in the boardroom. It felt natural for me to take over when he died. Plus, my grandfather loved to send me in to negotiate deals. He was convinced that men continue to underestimate women, even when they should know better. 'Dress beautifully, don't appear too intelligent, let the men think they have the upper hand, then go in for the kill.' It was great advice. I miss that man every day." I feel my heart break a little as those words fall out of my mouth. "My turn," I redirect. "How did you lose your eye?"

"I was a sniper, a sharpshooter, and a long-range sniper in Vietnam. I have two Purple Hearts, but I was discharged after losing my eye. I then worked in cybercrime at the FBI. Luckily, I found Dennis here in my retirement; he keeps me preoccupied. I need to stay busy to keep my mind away from the atrocities of war. Nothing I've ever done in the States can compare to what I've done or witnessed overseas in war. Those stories, unlike yours, won't be shared in a memoir; they'll die with me."

"How many people have you killed?"

"I won't say. That fact, that number, won't do any good for the world. It's better left unsaid. But I would bet it's less than the number of people that Big Sugar kills."

"For sure. Here's something you may not know about sugar. Sugar in a baby's brain is called ADHD. Sugar in an adult's brain is called dementia. Sugar in your eyes is called glaucoma. Sugar in your teeth is called cavities. Sugar in your sleep is called insomnia. Sugar in your blood is called diabetes, and excess sugar in your body is called cancer." I take a deep breath. Sugar sounds dastardly when I say all of this out loud. I feel slightly ashamed as I remind myself of the millions of dollars my family has profited from this enterprise for generations.

Bill claps back. "Yeah, but sugar on your tongue is delicious. You tell me these morbid facts *now* as we sip our twenty-ounce bottles of Mountain Dew with seventy-seven grams of sugar?"

"Yeah, well . . . this is a treat, not a habit. Everything delicious has consequences. Also, what's with the man bun?"

"That's two questions . . . but, if you must know, I haven't cut my hair since I came back from Vietnam."

"That's over fifty years ago."

"Yup, but I do trim it from time to time. When I let my hair down, it's a reminder of the distance in length and time between my two lives—a living reminder that life moves on . . . grows . . . it's a timeline of loss, lessons, each few inches a year, each wave a movement. But it's also a perfect hiding spot for damn near anything."

I smile. "You seem fine, having been through so much."

"Just because I carry it well doesn't mean it's not heavy," he says, patting his bun. "Literally and figuratively."

Barely fifteen minutes pass before we arrive back at the cemetery to find a somber trio of ladies.

"What's going on?"

"Dennis prefers that we don't discuss the case until we document our findings and meet officially next time," explains Filomena.

Estelle rushes to the clusia hedges and vomits. Filomena follows her, rubs her back, and wipes away a few droplets of saliva from her green tracksuit with a napkin.

Carol hands the dog back to Mr. Garrison.

"Is everything alright?" Mr. Garrison looks worried.

"Yes," Dennis assures him. "We'll handle this from here." Dennis texts our driver while discussing next steps with Mr. Garrison.

Mr. Garrison discreetly hands Dennis a thick white envelope while everyone diverts their eyes from the transaction. Dennis places the envelope inside his suit jacket pocket. Hmm. Strange.

My grandfather's voice pipes up in my head: Don't trust anyone who offers you money. Take the money, of course. But never trust them, and don't ever completely comply with their demands. Money is all about control. When you take the money, your adversary believes they've got the upper hand. They don't. All along, you've got the money and you own the next steps. Stay true to your goals and morals while pretending to follow the plan. Never be an ally. Never be a foe. Always keep them guessing about your true intentions.

Why I'm thinking about this right now, I have no idea. The envelope may contain pertinent information about the case, but I'll bet dollars to doughnuts that it's full of Benjamins.

When the minibus arrives, we all pile on, and Bill distributes water from the cooler to everyone. First he gives one to Estelle, who desperately needs to settle her stomach.

"Tell you what," Dennis offers, "let's stop for ice cream at the Celtic Creamery. I've got a hankerin' for some ice cream."

"Great idea," I say.

"I feel this case has been upsetting. I'm sorry; I was handed this case last night. The district attorney suggested I take a look at it, and I couldn't say no." Dennis rubs his head, looking at each of us one by one. "Is that alright with everyone? Ice cream and a chat before we head back?"

Everyone nods.

"That's fine by me. I just have to get back to the clinic by three," says Carol.

I order a cup of heavenly heath. The sisters choose yum yum bubble gum, Dennis selects coffee ice cream, and Carol and Bill opt for birthday cake.

Dennis hands two twenty-dollar bills to the cashier.

"I would have paid," Bill groans.

"You?" says Dennis. "You pinch a nickel until the buffalo shits."

"Funny. And not true." Bill defends himself. "I may be a little frugal with my own groceries and such, but never with the ladies. Never."

"I'll make the DA reimburse me for this. He owes me."

Once we're seated at the picnic table outside, Dennis says, "Alright, spit it out, everyone. Let's talk about it."

"I thought we don't talk about the case until everyone completes their research and it's all formally written down?" I ask.

"I can see that this case is disturbing to everyone, so let's have it. Tell me." Dennis jams his spoon in his ice cream, waiting for replies.

Carol is playing with her ice cream, moving it around in her cup. "I'll go first. The parents say Amos is the daughter's dog. That's a lie. That dog doesn't know the missing girl."

"What? What do you mean he doesn't know her? The file states that the dog was left behind at the graveside where the girl disappeared." Dennis opens the file and points to the paragraph where the dog is said to have been abandoned in the cemetery.

"Baloney! I handed him the shirt to sniff. He turned away; he couldn't care less. Earlier, the dog cowered at the stepmom's feet. This dog not only doesn't know the daughter but is also afraid of that woman." Carol takes a spoonful of ice cream and then glances over at the sisters for their opinion on the situation.

"She's not dead," Estelle blurts out. "Thank you for the ice cream, but I can't eat it. I feel nauseous."

Filomena explains, "I'll tell you why you feel nauseous, Estelle. I pulled the Four Swords, which signify being confined due to an illness, and drew the

Empress in reverse. A powerful woman exerting control over her. I believe the girl was being poisoned."

"That's a significant leap from a missing girl to a runaway who is being poisoned by her stepmother," suggests Bill.

"Well, she's not dead. The words I heard from the other side were 'belly ache' and 'I ran away.' " Estelle takes her ice cream and hands it to Bill. "You can have this."

"Thank you." Bill smiles at her. "I hope you feel better soon. I have Gas-X and some Pepto back home if you need it."

"I'm not sure that will help. But the feeling will subside. It always does." Estelle smiles back at Bill.

"The stepmother poisoning her stepdaughter reflects a case of Munchausen syndrome by proxy, similar to the infamous Gypsy Rose. The mother seeks attention for herself, intentionally harming her child or children to achieve that. Sometimes it's out of love. Other times it's for money. It's truly disturbing," I say. I quickly look up Gypsy Rose Blanchard on my iPhone and copy and paste the article I find to the group. "So sad if this is true."

"How do you know so much about this?" Carol asks me.

"I was really intrigued by Gypsy Rose's story when it broke. It's hard to imagine any mother could do such a thing to her own child," I say. "I've since watched all the movies and documentaries, and now she has a reality television show."

"Let's discuss next steps," Dennis says. "I'll have my team at the station check local shelters and churches where a runaway might go."

Bill offers, "I'll check social media. If the dog we met today isn't her dog, Amos, then maybe she is with the real Amos."

"Why would her parents lie about the dog?" asks Carol.

"I'm going to guess for credibility, so it doesn't seem like a sixteen-year-old girl's runaway story. If a dog was left behind, something more sinister must have happened, so more resources would be allocated to the case. Just my hypothesis," suggests Dennis.

"I can check wellness centers such as yoga retreats and rehab centers. She may have gone there, especially if her body needed healing—both body and mind. Those places tend to be more secretive and cater to a more selective clientele that can afford their services. I know the owners of a few retreats, so I'll make some calls," I offer.

Filomena proposes, "What are the chances of unearthing her sister's grave to check for poison?"

"None, without proof or consent from the parents," Dennis groans.

"What was the sister's official cause of death?" Filomena points to the file.

Dennis replies, "Pneumonia."

I offer my knowledge of Munchausen syndrome to say, "My guess is that her stepmother made her so ill that it weakened her immune system to the point where pneumonia ultimately killed her."

Dennis sends a message to the minibus driver to pick us up. "Alright, folks, wrap it up. There's work to do. We'll reconvene sometime next week."

I have a bright idea and suggest, "I'm going to call my Realtor. He's lived around here since the seventies. I'm sure he could tell me a story or two about the Garrison family. I'll see what I can find out."

"Great idea. Small town. Few secrets." Bill collects the empty cups and cleans the table.

The color is starting to return to Estelle's face. She looks much improved.

My ankle is itchy. I look down at my left ankle. Four swollen red bumps. Ugh. "Oh no! Mosquito bites," I yelp. "I hate mosquitoes. Pesky little blood-sucking buggers."

"You know, it's only the women mosquitoes that steal your blood. It's for their young." Estelle scratches her ankles now too.

"Murderous, wretched thieves," I scold.

"Use Preparation H when you get home," Bill suggests. "Works wonders for an itch."

"What makes you think I have hemorrhoids?" I say.

"At our age, everyone has hemorrhoids . . . hey, you ever wonder what ever happened to Preparation A through G?" Bill scratches his head.

"Is anyone going to the Rednecks and Renegades shindig tomorrow night at the country club?" asks Estelle.

"Yes," says Carol. "Are you dressing up as a redneck or a renegade?"

"Haven't decided." Estelle shrugs.

Dennis swings a fake lasso around his head and exclaims, "Saddle up, partners, for some line dancing, hayrides, beer pong, and mechanical bull riding . . . yeehaw!"

I protest, "Oh, bless that big bald head of yours, but I won't be caught dead on a mechanical bull."

Bill chuckles. "We will see about that."

Chapter Fourteen

Diana
Rednecks & Renegades

What on God's green Earth does a gal wear to a redneck jamboree? I'll have to consult Rebecca; she'll know what to do.

By 5 p.m. Rebecca arrives with four outfits in hand. I toss the one made of cowhide onto the couch. "Nope. Too much!"

I strut around the townhouse in three ensembles, putting on a fashion show for Rebecca's approval. It's strange because when I stand in front of a mirror, it clearly reveals a seventy-four-year-old woman. Inside, however, I feel thirty-three, or I could choose any age from my thirties; they were all wonderful. My gray hair and a spattering of random wrinkles betray my youthful sense of self. It's an aging thing; the youngsters wouldn't understand. As you age, the outer shell never matches the youth within.

I select the long-sleeve brown suede jumpsuit featuring a V-neck and leather fringe details. I match the jumpsuit with cowboy booties and suede tassel earrings.

"I'm not entirely sure what I'm in for, but I'm ready for it," I say aloud.

"You look fabulous." Rebecca beams. She's great for my ego. I'd have her accompany me everywhere if I could.

"I can't thank you enough," I say. "You're the best!" I hug her, then she grabs her purse and dashes out the door as quickly as any twenty-something would, escaping her boss on a Saturday evening.

When I arrive, the country club is completely transformed into an old-time saloon. I'm astounded by the budget that the activities committee must have to host such an event. A giant deer antler chandelier looms large in the center of the room. The scent of barbecue fills the air, the most requested choice for dinner. The wooden bar stretches long enough to comfortably accommodate twenty-five people in wooden saloon barstools.

Neon lights flicker over rows of whiskey bottles as a drunken man dressed like Elvis Presley—white jumpsuit, rhinestones, and all—stumbles onto the twenty-by-twenty LED-starlit, color-changing dance floor. With a tipsy grin and a half-empty beer in hand, he tries to join the ladies in the line dance. His hips swing and sway slightly out of sync with the music. His sequined cape flares dramatically, spinning in the wrong direction, and he nearly topples into a group of men in jeans and cowboy hats. Instead of helping him find a seat, they prop him back up. Undeterred, Elvis stumbles through "Boot Scootin' Boogie" and makes his way to the center of the dance floor for a final Elvis pose, left leg stretched, right arm raised, as he yelps, "Thank you, thank you very much!" The residents applaud.

Geez, what a spectacle! It's too bad the gang missed this. Where are they? I glance around the room and spot Filomena and Estelle at the bar. The sight of the sisters always brightens my mood. These ladies are like human medicine. An hour with them would make anyone feel fabulous. I'm happy we're friends and lucky they chose *me* to be part of their cold case crime club.

"Hey, did you see the entertainment?" I ask Filomena.

"Yeah, that's our resident Elvis. He's a real hoot." She and Estelle tap their shot glasses and slam back a shot of whiskey like nobody's business. They're matching tonight, of course, in white lace dresses and cowboy hats.

"You both look lovely. Do you always dress similarly?"

"Yes, twin rules. Our husbands did as well."

"What?"

"They didn't dress like us, of course, but they dressed similarly to each other for special occasions, just for fun. They were great guys, and I miss them." Filomena makes a playful pouty face.

"Nice face," says Estelle.

"What am I missing? I'm confused. What happened to your husbands?"

Estelle orders three shots of Jameson and says, "We left them a few years ago. We'd been with our husbands since high school; it was time to move on and live a little before we die."

"I understand completely. So you're both single now?"

Filomena says as the shots arrive, "We're both in a relationship with freedom."

"Hear, hear, sister," I say. Whoo, leaning against the bar, pounding shots, attending a country jamboree? Who am I?

Before long, Dennis arrives with Bill, both dressed like Hells Angels.

"Guessing redneck," I say, dripping in sarcasm.

"Funny. I'm a Florida redneck every day. Today I'm one of the most notorious outlaws."

"How are you going to dance with those doodads on your boots?" asks Estelle.

"Oh, these are spikes," he clarifies, lifting his boot to show them off. "Cowboys have spurs, renegades have spikes. Carefully, I suppose."

Filomena laments, "Be careful then. Don't injure the elderly."

The activities director is out on the dance floor teaching people the line dance to "A Bar Song" when we hear screams coming from across the dance floor. We whirl our heads around to see Carol holding onto the mechanical bull for dear life. She's screaming, and then suddenly a siren goes off above the bull, and the lights flicker. She gets off the bull just as we arrive, and she is rewarded with a hundred-dollar gift card to Crawdaddy's, our local New Orleans-style Cajun restaurant.

"Impressive," says Dennis. "How long were you up there?"

"Nine seconds. They say it's a record." Carol is out of breath. She leans over, grabbing her knees for support. "I'm going to need a stiff drink after that."

Bill gives her the cowboy hat that had flown off her head during the ride.

"Thank you." She smiles.

"I didn't know you were so agile," Bill says, raising his eyebrows playfully.

"Don't get any ideas, cowboy," Carol teases.

"Um, renegade, not cowboy," he points out.

"Right." Carol puts on her cowboy hat, looking nice all dressed up in jeans, boots, and a bedazzled cowboy shirt. I've only ever seen her in scrubs.

After a few more rounds of drinks, we all head to the dance floor.

Bill shouts out to Estelle, "I can see your bloomers through your dress."

"Bill, no one says bloomers anymore."

"Panties, then."

"Worse, cringe. Bill, stop! How do you know that's not the look I'm going for? It's a white dress. Of course you're going to see them. Don't you like my lace lingerie?" she says playfully, shooting Bill a devilish smile.

"Oh, lingerie? Yes, it's lovely," he admits.

The line dances are easy to pick up. Dare I say, I'm having the most fun I can remember in a long time. There's definitely something to this country music line dancing thing.

The barbecue food is exquisite. Our chef did an outstanding job. Mr. Anderson, our resident cat, sits patiently by the dessert table all night until Carol offers him a slice of Key lime pie toward the end of the evening. He nuzzles against her in gratitude for her kindness.

After three more shots of whiskey, I end the night on the mechanical bull, but I last only three seconds. Never in a hundred years did I ever think I would ride a mechanical bull. But Bill was right. He told me so. I'll give him credit for that.

Along the path home through the park, I stumble across a worn brown leather bag. A soft voice in my mind tells me not to open it. Walk away, Diana. Go home. I don't listen. I open the flashlight app on my iPhone. Someone must have dropped the bag here accidentally. It looks out of place, set on top of a patch of saw grass by the edge of the creek.

A green lizard crawls out from beneath it, craning its neck in my direction, then runs off. I scoop up the bag carefully. My legs are jelly—must be from the mechanical horse? I feel woozy. I sit on the bench and peel open the zipper. It's packed with syringes—many different sizes. Vials of medicine are hidden below. Ketamine, propofol, and morphine.

"What in tarnation?"

Chapter Fifteen

Theo

They say the average person will hop from job to job about ten to twelve times before settling on a job they love and a career they're proud of—or at least one that earns enough money to make them proud of their choice. The proverbial game of life is a continuous series of rolling dice, moving your pawn across the squares, and making pivotal choices that seem minor at the time. But go back, reroll the dice, land on a different square, make an unconventional career choice, and voilà, your life is vastly different. Life is full of choices. Choose wisely. It will make or break you in the end.

My first job was uneventful, so I'll tell you about my second. I was working as a teacher's assistant, a TA, pursuing my doctorate when I discovered love letters in my professor's coat closet. A squeaky floorboard may not be suspicious to most people, but most people are not me. I don't trust most people in general, so a squeaky floor plank in the coat closet screamed that something sinister was happening to me. Of course, I bent down to investigate. Lo and behold, the wooden plank popped right out, and a pack of letters written to young ladies by my dear professor looked back at me, begging for my eyes to read.

Here we go again. Shit rolls downhill, and it always finds *ME*.

Dear Reader,

January 14, 1981

As January ushers in a new semester, professors hire TAs to assist with grading, logging, and tracking papers and exams. It's an easy enough job—time-consuming and tedious, sure, but not difficult.

I hadn't been on the job for more than a week when I stumbled upon a treasure trove of love letters from the professor addressed to some women in his Intro to Law class. Initially, they seem innocent enough: You're beautiful, perhaps we can meet for lunch one day, etc. Nothing too nefarious.

The professor, I might add, is only maybe ten years their senior. It was not unheard of in those days to meet up with your professor from time to time to discuss classroom topics. Also, not out of the ordinary to date outside the classroom once the class has commenced. So, at first glance, the man is a pervert. He likes young women. Read further, and the letters take a darker turn. Meet me at the cabin on Saturday, or expect a failing grade. Join me or expect a phone call from me to your boyfriend. One note read Meet me tonight, or you'll never see your dog, Twinkie, again. This is just grand. Now I feel compelled to get involved.

I have no romantic feelings for either sex. I've dated both men and women in my youth; it was more of a science experiment, if I'm being honest. Yuck to both. Maybe my mom dropped me on my head when I was a small child. There's no way to know, because, as I mentioned, my mom is dead. Getting involved is neither chivalry nor a way to take down the patriarchy. I'm just going to follow the facts and do what I believe I was born to do: remove scum from the Earth.

I spent several weeks monitoring the professor's interactions with his female students. One student named Linda dropped out of the class mid-semester. I tracked her down. I listened intently to her story. He wooed her. He wined and dined her. Then blackmailed her. He took naked photos of her while she was asleep. Then he promised to place the photos around campus unless she paid him money for them.

So, that following weekend, I visited his cabin. I discovered a stash of money, which I removed from the premises. I repaid Linda and ensured she returned the money to the other girls as well, anonymously of course. I did what needed to be done. You'll know where to find him, but I'm uncertain if anyone ever has. Just listen for the squeaky floorboards.

Chapter Sixteen

Mr. Anderson

I prance by Tom in the garden this morning, feeding a carrot to a gopher tortoise. The wildlife around here is very well-fed by the residents and staff. There's something about old age and caring for outdoor creatures. There must be a scientific study somewhere on why older folks, those over fifty, tend to feed and care for these critters, while younger people, today's youth under fifty, walk right by without acknowledging their existence. I would guess that the contrast between older folks and younger ones is a popular topic in every fifty-five plus community. No generation can ever fully understand its youth. It seems to be a human condition. In the animal world, it's evolve or die, but humans must operate by different rules. The Great Divide: The Wrinklies v The Whippersnappers. Wouldn't this make for a great television show? I'd watch it.

"Hello, Mr. Anderson. You're late today. Where have you been?" Tom asks me.

"Sorry I'm late, but I had to rescue an old lady who got stuck in a tree," I muse sarcastically, stomping my tail and twitching my whiskers. All he hears is, "Meow."

"Oh, I see." Tom pats my head. "You were busy this morning chasing mice. Good boy!"

My humor is wasted on humans. I don't know why I bother chatting with them at all.

Tom's dying. I can smell his body's decay. If death has a scent, I would describe it like bikers eating breakfast. It smells to me like leather and maple syrup. It hits the olfactory nerves harshly and makes my whiskers tingle. Humans can't detect death like the animal kingdom. Heck, vultures hover for days, awaiting the exact moment the soul leaves the body, and only the nutrient-rich carcass remains to begin their feast.

Carol arrives shortly after and sits beside Tom on the bench. I'm not a fan of this relationship. I don't like those two spending so much time together in the mornings. Don't get me wrong; I'm not attracted to human women. Carol is beautiful to me—she has a beautiful soul. She's been a disheveled mess lately and smells like Monty's old shoe closet. I'm worried about her. It must be job stress. It's flu season, and the clinic has been bustling with sick people lately.

Carol reaches over and rubs my belly. The world fades away, and suddenly I can hear Karen Carpenter singing "Top of the World" in my head while I lie here in ecstasy, caressed by my favorite human.

"Come by the clinic later, Mr. Anderson. I've got some catnip for you," Carol promises.

Tom leans over and whispers something in Carol's ear. All I can make out is "after dinner" and "text me."

Chapter Seventeen

Diana
Finding Vanessa & Amos

I tell no one about the leather bag I found at the creek. Something inside me suggests I keep this to myself for now. I hide it behind the tea canister in the kitchen cupboard for now.

A week passes before Dennis is ready to meet again to discuss the case. This morning I'm greeted by a bird. A male painted bunting is enjoying seeds from my bird feeder on my back porch. What a beautiful songbird! He has such vibrant purple, red, and yellow feathers. Every creature in nature has a universal message for you, should you choose to acknowledge or believe such things. My painted bunting friend reminds me to add color to my life, which I have done with the motley crew of characters I've been spending time with lately. Colorful indeed!

I'm greeted by Tom at the country club door. "Good morning." He smiles so wide that his perfectly white veneers blind me. Wow, he must have spent a fortune on those. His smile is beautiful; I never noticed until now. The contrast between his ultrawhite teeth and his peppery, full head of hair makes him stand out like an older male model. How have I not realized how good-looking this man is?

The other men don't like him. Bill once referred to him as a human impersonation of a kidney stone. My first impression was that he was too chatty and overly friendly. My gut reaction to people who try too hard is that they are hiding their true selves beneath their masks. He is easy on the eyes, however. What do the kids say these days . . . oh yes, he's eye candy.

Suddenly my daughter's voice echoes in my mind: The last thing you need right now is a new man in your life. She's right. I refocus and walk toward Filomena, who is already seated at a round table by the garden window.

"Hello, Filomena." I smile and sit down.

"I saw how you were looking at Tom." She winks at me.

"Oh. To be honest, I never really noticed how good-looking he is. Usually, he's annoying. Bothersome, like split ends or clogged pores. I never gave him the once-over until today."

"He's popular around here with the ladies," she warns. "If you know what I mean."

"No. I don't. Spill the beans." I lean in closer, thoroughly intrigued by what she's about to say.

"My understanding is that he has a decent-sized pecker. But never mind that. It works! On command! All the time!" Filomena adjusts a loose hair and places it behind her ear. She blushes.

"Oh . . . oh. You and him?"

"Well, maybe once . . . or twice. My sister hooked up with him once too."

"Really?"

"Really."

Estelle pulls out a chair to sit down, startling us with a screech. "What are you two chatting about?" she asks.

"Just a little Tomfoolery." Filomena blurts out a laugh, and I join her.

"Oh. Yes. Tom . . ." Estelle winks. "Don't tell the guys. They're the jealous type."

I gesture, zipping up my lip and throwing away the key.

"Who's making the morning cocktails today?" Estelle asks.

"Can I make them?"

"Sure," Estelle and Filomena answer together.

"Do we have RumChata?" I look past them toward the coffee station.

"No idea," says Estelle.

"Never mind, I'll have Jeb bring some in from the bar in the Bentley."

"Talking about hunks. That Jeb is a six-foot-four hunk of burning love, if you ask me. He looks like a clean-cut Jason Momoa. He looks more like a bodyguard than a driver. Also . . . I'm single."

"He's probably my best friend; I don't pimp him out, sorry. Jason Momoa, huh? Hmm. I'll be right back."

Within ten minutes, I've made everyone RumChata coffees.

"Let me help you with these." Bill appears at the coffee station to help serve the group.

"Ooh la la . . . what is this?" asks Filomena.

"It's RumChata coffee. Coffee, a shot of RumChata, and whipped cream for aesthetics. I pair my coffee drinks with Nilla Wafers from my friends at Nabisco, centered nicely in the whipped cream."

I hand a mug to Filomena first. Her mug reads "I like my men how I like my coffee. Sliding off the roof of my car."

"I love this one. This mug must be new."

I hand Estelle a mug that reads "Witches Brew." She takes a sip. "Hints of vanilla and cinnamon. Very tasty."

"Thank you. I saw this concoction on Instagram, and I loved it." I place my mug beside my cell phone. The mug message reads "Nope. Not today. Walk away."

Bill places his mug and Dennis's on the table. Dennis's mug features an image of a doughnut and the message "Eat more hole foods."

"This is my mug. I brought it here from the office," Dennis points out.

Bill hides his mug from everyone at the table. He takes a seat and reads his mug aloud. "The world hasn't been the same since Prince died."

"Hear, hear," cheers Dennis.

We all clink glasses and enjoy our morning coffee.

"Where's Carol?" I ask.

"She's always late." Bill looks toward the entrance. "She'll show up soon, I'm sure."

Dennis rolls his big leather chair away from the table and retrieves Vanessa's file from his briefcase. The air is tense enough to choke on. We wait in anticipation. Every pair of eyes is pinned on him.

"Let's do a recap. Estelle and Filomena believe she ran away. She may or may not have been poisoned or mistreated in some way. It was suggested that the dog we saw last week was not her dog, Amos. It was also suggested that her late sister may have been poisoned as well. Bill, what do you have to report?"

Bill pulls a folded envelope from his pants pocket and places it on the table. "I found out that the dog was adopted from the Humane Society of the Treasure Coast the day Vanessa went missing."

"So instead of contacting the police to find their daughter, they rushed out to adopt a new dog?" Dennis questions.

"Seems so." Bill nods.

"Suspicious." Dennis scratches a note into his file.

"I'll go next," I say excitedly. "I called a friend of mine who owns several rehabilitation centers in Central and Southern Florida. She said she would look into trying to find her. Last night she got back to me. Vanessa spent six months right under everyone's noses at The Recovery Village in Jensen Beach. This is not one of my friend's facilities, but she knows the people who run it. Of course, those records are confidential, and I'm not supposed to know that Vanessa spent time there, but . . . there you have it. Maybe you can get a warrant to subpoena those records?"

A sigh of relief comes from both Filomena and Estelle.

"At least we know she's not dead." Filomena sips her coffee and takes a bite of the Nilla Wafer. "Delicious."

"Thank God for small mercies," Estelle says, looking past me toward the entrance. "Carol is here."

When Carol approaches the table, she apologizes for being late.

"You don't look well." Bill pulls out a chair for Carol to sit.

"I can't stay. I might be coming down with something. I'm going home to lie down." She places her envelope on the table. "Her dog, Amos, attends Sandy Paws Day Spa a few days a week. I found him there. He sniffed her shirt and perked right up. I waited in the parking lot, and Vanessa picked him up at four p.m. So if you'd like to speak with her, you know where to find her." Carol coughs. "Excuse me, please. Good luck." She turns and walks away.

"Oh, poor Carol. She's been working so many hours lately; no wonder she's sick." Estelle opens our group chat and sends a get-well-soon text to Carol.

"One more thing." Bill lifts his pointer finger. "Mrs. Garrison. Her name before marriage was Adele Bunting."

I nearly spit out my coffee, thinking about the painted bunting that visited my bird feeder this morning. Is this a message from the universe? My grandfather's voice resonates in my mind: Pay attention to the details. Nature's voice is loud. He would walk through the sugar fields daily, allowing the sugarcane to tell him what it needed—water, nutrients, pesticides. The sound of church bells in the distance is a sign that is not lost on me.

"What about her? We conducted a comprehensive background check on her," Dennis says as he flips through the file to Adele's information. "She was a teacher at South Fork High School. The staff reported that she was a strict teacher, but nothing unusual stood out to anyone. She taught algebra."

"Yes," Bill says, "but according to my research, she was also the head of the agricultural club. Perhaps we should examine the types of pesticides used at the school."

"Good idea. I'll get a few badges to work on this in the office," Dennis promises. "Maybe this could lead to exhuming the sister's body."

"Someone should also check on Mr. Garrison's health," I suggest. "If Mrs. Garrison has indeed poisoned her stepdaughters, what makes us think she'll stop there?"

Chapter Eighteen

Diana
Game Night

Thunder rumbles nearby. The daylight has all been whiled away. Not much is happening around campus tonight. At 7 p.m. the country club is offering Painting with a Twist. For fifty dollars, you get chips, salsa, two glasses of wine, and a canvas to paint the full moon over the shores of Jensen Beach with the assistance of the art director. It sounds fun, but art has never piqued my interest. I find myself as bored as a rat in a cage. I've got to keep myself busy so I don't eat my way through the pantry out of boredom. Extra pounds don't come off easily after menopause. I decide to call Jeb.

"Hello, Diana." He answers on the first ring. "Where would you like to go this evening?"

"I don't know. I'm restless. Somewhere I've never been. Surprise me."

"On my way now. See you in five minutes. Bring a raincoat; it seems like we're going to get a soaker soon."

When Jeb arrives in the Bentley, it's sprinkling, and he greets me with an umbrella. I immediately notice he is wearing the cologne I gave him last Christmas. I can't remember the name, but I know it's from Dior.

I take a sip of the champagne he pours for me once I am settled. A small bowl of Nilla Wafers sits beside my glass of champagne. He knows me so well. "You smell fabulous." I absolutely love a man who smells delicious.

"A gift from a friend," he says.

"A friend?" I question.

"My best friend," he answers and winks in the rearview mirror.

"Yes, we are, aren't we? How long have you been driving for me, Jeb?"

"I've been with you through your first days at the company, all four of your marriages, your grandfather's funeral, the raising of the beautiful Lola, and now your granddaughter Lydia—all the milestones that bring us right up to today."

Five marriages, actually. I don't correct him. Not many people know I ran off to Las Vegas a week after graduating from college to marry my jerk-off frat boy boyfriend. My mother had it annulled within a week. I haven't thought about that in a while. Memories are a funny thing. They're always there, lingering, waiting to be triggered. I wish I could bury that memory forever. One day some brilliant scientist will discover a method to destroy specific unsettling memories and enhance others, maybe even manufacture a few fun, fake memories—who cares as long as they bring joy? One can only wish.

"The first days at the company, that's right," I say. "That takes us back to 1969. That's really something, isn't it? That's fifty-six years ago."

"It certainly is." He nods, glancing back at me in the mirror.

"I've also witnessed *your* life events, including your wedding, your son's birth, his medical school graduation, and the passing of your beloved Susan. I truly liked her; she was such a sweet soul. I hope you feel blessed to have known such a wonderful woman who brought you so much joy for so many years."

"Yes, she truly was a sweet soul. I was fortunate to have found her. However, through all these many years, you and I still maintain our friendship. I cherish our bond just as much as I value my marriage to Susan."

I smile. A big, wide, happy smile. He is my most cherished friend and an essential part of my life. I don't say this, but I genuinely feel it. No one knows me better than Jeb. No one has seen all of me like he has—the laughter, the tears, the fits of rage. You can't hide your emotions trapped in the back seat of a car when the proverbial shit hits the fan. Jeb has always been there for me with kind words and great advice. For that, he will hold a special place in my heart forever. I make a special note on my phone to ensure I dedicate my memoir to Jeb, my best friend.

Ten minutes later, we arrive at Play Money Arcade. "Where are we?" I look around and can't imagine why we stopped here, in the middle of a strip mall in Stuart.

"We're at the arcade."

"An arcade? Aren't we too old for that? Aren't arcades for kids?"

"My dear Diana, there is no defined age for pinball."

"Pinball? Heavens to Betsy . . . I don't think I've ever played pinball. What possessed you to bring me here?"

"My idea is twofold. You mentioned that you wanted to visit somewhere new, and I believe this could be a fun place to bring Lydia. Lord knows there isn't much for kids to do in this area besides the beach and the children's museum."

"Great idea, Jeb. Thank you! You never disappoint. Now that I think about it, you might be one of the few people in my life who has never let me down."

"Alright, Diana, don't pressure me like that. The night is young, and I have hours to find ways to drive you into an intense emotional frenzy. Let's just go have some fun like we're kids again."

I walk cautiously into the arcade. It feels like stepping into a different realm filled with flashing neon lights, pulsating music from the seventies, and a vast array of assorted dings and dongs. When I look past the cashier, I immediately notice a claw machine and an air hockey table. I mentally note these games that Lydia will genuinely enjoy playing.

A row of pinball machines stands before us, and we settle on Elvira's House of Horrors. Elvira's two-story mansion is centered in the playfield, challenging the ball to enter. I go first and launch the small silver ball onto the vibrant playfield, and a surge of anticipation courses through me. The machine comes alive with dazzling lights, sounds, and intricate mechanical movements, captivating all my senses. When the ball falls toward me, I grip the flipper buttons and hit it. It ricochets unpredictably, striking different targets and generating loud sounds.

The score above changes rapidly. I lean into the machine, pressing the flipper buttons hard, doing my best to prevent the ball from rolling into the gutter. When the ball finally escapes, I feel exhilarated. The scoreboard rewards me with 230 thousand points, and while I don't fully grasp whether that's a good score or a bad one, wow . . . what a rush!

"You've got some great reflexes there. Impressive."

"Thank you, Jeb. Your turn."

"Oh, no. I'm not so good at pinball. Skee-Ball is more my speed. You go again. You get three tries," he explains.

"No, Jeb. You go. Let's see what kind of reflexes you've got."

"Alrighty then. How about this: If I beat your two hundred and thirty thousand this round—and remember, I'm terrible at pinball—but just in case, you'll have to agree to let me take you out on a date. A real date."

"A date? Us, on a real date? What do you mean?"

"Just this. I'll spit it out," he says confidently, seemingly well-rehearsed. "I'm retiring from the company at the end of February. Like you, I've been with the company for a long time, and it's time to enjoy my senior years." He pauses and swallows hard.

"I've wanted to retire for quite some time; I just didn't know how to walk away from *you*. So I'm asking . . . when I retire, can we go on a date?" As big and manly as Jeb is, his cheeks flush. He's afraid of my response. This may be the most vulnerable behavior I've witnessed from him.

"Jeb, you've caught me off guard here. Why me? I'm a terrible choice. I have a horrible track record. You know this better than anyone."

"That's exactly it. I know you well, and you know me well. I believe we would make good companions for one another, that's all. What do you say?"

"Well, yes. Um. Perhaps. Let's see how your pinball round unfolds."

Jeb nestles up to the machine, looks toward me, smiles, and pulls the plunger. The mini cannonball shoots off to smash its targets. The entire playfield lights up like a fireworks display at Magic Kingdom. Several times, the ball attempts to escape, but Jeb skillfully manages to keep it in play, plunging his hip into the machine and, at other times, lifting a leg for extra leverage, adding more perceived power to the mechanical flippers. The ball enters Elvira's mansion twice, illuminating the house like blinking Christmas lights. This man is playing for keeps. When the ball finally falls into the galley, he gains over 2,537,000 additional points to our score.

"I did it!" He throws both arms into the air.

"I feel as if you pinball sharked me. You told me you weren't good at pinball, yet you absolutely killed it! I've been hornswoggled."

"I've learned a thing or two about manipulation from you." He smirks.

"Manipulation? I suppose you mean my beguiling charm?" I say with a wink.

"Yes, exactly that."

"Well, congratulations." My heart pounds heavily in my chest. I feel empowered, adventurous, and unstoppable. Suddenly my world goes silent, and the only sound I hear in this noisy establishment is the thunder of my racing heart. Our eyes meet, and I feel a flutter in my stomach. Instinctively, I pull him close and kiss him as if it's the day before the apocalypse, and there's nothing left to lose.

Chapter Nineteen

Diana
The Ambulance

Sleep is abruptly shattered by a distant piercing wail. The sun has yet to rise. An ambulance's siren crescendos outside, stinging my ears. My elderly eardrums get more delicate year after year. The ambulance is a reminder that death is near. My grandfather used to say that if the devil comes knocking at your door, chances are you flirted with him at the dance. Of course this is a metaphor, but at age sixteen, I took this literally. Today, if the devil came knocking, he'd be greeted with a Smith & Wesson and instant regret that he stopped at the wrong house.

I reach beside me. I feel only cold sheets and emptiness where Jeb should be. He's gone. Last night's memory is a pleasant blur. My stomach flutters —butterflies, love's first sign. Conflicting feelings of passion and loneliness hit me all at once. I close my eyes momentarily to reminisce. It's been a long time since I felt emotions so strong. I look toward the nightstand. There's a note.

The blaring sound of the ambulance is moving closer. My heart races and a sense of urgency fills the air. The clock reads 6:10 a.m. The note will have to wait until later. I want to read it now, but I'm not in the right headspace currently. Something terrible is looming.

I shuffle briskly out of bed to get dressed. A strange sense of dread comes over me. A knot forms in my empty stomach, tying the dread together in an unsettling bow. Red lights flicker through my kitchen window. Faces peek out between gaps in the curtains of neighboring homes. As I'm pouring myself a quick cup of coffee, Dennis comes through with a group text.

Meet me at the entrance. Ziggy is dead.

Chapter Twenty

Theo

Ziggy had to die. Some people never learn. It's true what they say: Only the good die young. My mom is a good example of that scenario. Ziggy had plenty of years to correct the error of his ways. Nope. Even at his age, with a plethora of drugs and a penis that barely stands erect, he still couldn't stop himself.

Typically, pedophiles are easy to spot. They don't even try to hide it. They're almost always men who have never been married. They've never been in a serious relationship. They seem a bit off in many ways, and people generally don't seem to like them.

Florida is a haven for these men. Who can blame them? Beautiful weather and long days are enticing. The real draw is that Floridians are transient. People move here from all different places and don't tend to stay in their homes for very long before moving along to another place. You never establish a real sense of community in any given area. People change homes like toddlers change underwear. In this respect, neighbors are never really invested in looking out for one another. No one is paying close attention to their surroundings. It's not hard to snatch a kid without anyone paying too close attention.

By the time pedos move into a fifty-five plus community, they let their guard down, but I know how to spot them. These folks rarely change their ways. Later in life, they get complacent and sloppy. I hadn't lived here for two days before meeting Stanley. I knew what I had to do to rid The Ocean's Edge of the likes of him. It was a shame that Monty got caught in the crosshairs. That was unintentional. I really wish I didn't have to kill Monty. He was really well-liked around here.

I wish it didn't always have to be me. Some people live their entire lives without ever witnessing a crime. I, on the other hand, *always* seem to be in the line of fire. Over and over again, it's me who has to put a stop to the evils before me. So, once more, I answer God's call and do what I do best.

Dear Reader,

February 7, 2025
I originally intended to tell my story chronologically, but certain circumstances have

arrived upon my doorstep that compel me to write about them in real time.

Last week, I saw Ziggy wobbling down the park path, his steps unsteady and his eyes unfocused. He chuckled to himself, muttering incoherent thoughts. I followed him to ensure he got home safely.

When I arrived, he stumbled up the stairs and fell onto the stoop to catch his breath. I decided to help him up and into his house. I had placed him in his leather recliner chair in the living room and poured a glass of water from the kitchen when I heard voices coming from a room off the dining room.

I tried to hand the water to Ziggy, but he was fast asleep. I ventured off toward the room with the voices and found his computer playing a looping recording of a kindergarten classroom. I glanced at his bookcase and discovered hundreds of labeled tapes dating back five years. Beside the computer was a sixteen-ounce bottle of pink cherry water-based lubricant. Beneath his desk, a wastebasket overflowed with nasty, wadded-up paper towels—disgusting.

Tonight, while the residents were occupied at the country club attending an art class, I slipped into Ziggy's apartment and did what had to be done.

Chapter Twenty-One

Mr. Anderson

In the midst of my evening stroll, I pause mid-step beneath Ziggy's window. My ears twitch. Something is wrong. The scent coming from Ziggy's bedroom is familiar but . . . off. Stale. I let my whiskers sniff the air, then jump into the open window and onto Ziggy's bed. His room smells like a lumberjack's laundry basket. That scent is mixed with a familiar scent of death—leather and waffles.

I nudge Ziggy's arm with my nose and wait. He doesn't respond. I say, "Hey, get up. Are you alright? You smell bad," or, "Meow," as he might hear.

I lick his ear. Maybe that'll wake him. That's when I notice a needle mark behind his ear—the same one I found on Monty the night he died. There's a pillow on the floor. Two plus two equals four, and even a cat can tell that Ziggy was murdered the same way Monty was killed, although no one noticed the mark behind Monty's ear.

When elderly individuals die, few ask too many questions. They often pass away in their sleep, don't they? Autopsies are popular on TV and in movies, but in real life, they cost five to seven thousand dollars. Family members rarely agree to cover these expenses. The police also won't fund them unless there is tangible proof of homicide, especially given the statewide budget cuts these days. I hear an ambulance in the distance and greet the medics at the door when they arrive. I need to learn as much as I can about how Ziggy died and find a way to tell Carol about it. These deaths are connected. I know this for sure—call it cat intuition.

Truth be told, I didn't care much for Ziggy; he was a strange bird. But I'll do whatever I must to find out who killed Monty and avenge his death.

Chapter Twenty-Two

Diana
What Happened to Ziggy?

As I approach the ambulance, the medics roll the gurney onto the back. A white sheet covers the silhouette of a human body. They slam the doors shut and drive away. The side-view mirrors mock me as they descend the driveway. Objects in the mirror are closer than they seem, a message that resonates.

"What took you so long to get here? You almost missed the whole spectacle!" Bill pulls a pencil from his man bun and scribbles a note in a small notebook. I lean over and read *6:32. Diana arrives.*

"Seriously, Bill? Am I a suspect? What leads you to believe there was foul play? For the love of murder . . . me? Really? Come on now!"

"I'm just trying to be thorough, that's all," Bill explains.

"How was your evening with Jeb?" Dennis asks with a devilish smile. "I noticed he left very early this morning."

"Can't a gal have any privacy in this place? Please make better use of your detective stalking skills."

"A stalker? What did I miss now?" Estelle asks. Both Estelle and Filomena are out of breath when they arrive.

Bill recaps the conversation. "Ziggy is dead. There's no clear indication of how, and Diana had a late-night gentleman caller."

"Do tell," says Filomena.

"Alright, stop it! Jeb spent the night if you must know. We've been friends for almost sixty years." Wow, that sounds like forever saying it out loud. "I have nothing further to add."

"Understood. Leave her alone, fellas," Filomena says with a harsh look that implies another word about it, and someone's gonna get hurt.

"So what now?" Estelle removes her glasses and wipes them with her T-shirt to remove the residue from the morning mist. Filomena follows suit. Today their eyewear is red, matching their red tracksuits. I wonder if they possess glasses in every color to coordinate with their outfits.

Dennis says, "I'm going to the coroner this morning. I want to make sure the body has no visible signs of foul play. Monty died the same way—in his sleep—and so did Henry, a few weeks before Monty."

"Who is Henry?" I ask, trying to keep up with the neighborhood death count.

"Henry was our neighborhood chess champion," Filomena explains. "He would sit in the country club lobby all day, waiting to challenge the neighbors to a game of chess. To my recollection, he never lost. People were determined, however, to beat him at his game at least once. I don't believe anyone ever got the chance. The administration loved him because people would throw plenty of f-bombs, and the HOA would charge exorbitant public nuisance penalty fees to the perpetrators. He was Ocean's Edge's cash cow. I'm sure they miss him."

"Well, now they have me." Bill opens a twice-folded bill from his pants pocket. "I have a four-hundred-dollar fine that's due at the end of the month with seventeen links attached."

"What did you do now, Bill?" Dennis asks.

"Not me. My grandkids are boys aged four, six, and seven. I suppose my daughter told the kids not to swear on the property during their last visit. Well, they must have taken this as a challenge. Every opportunity they get, walking past a surveillance camera, they're recorded screaming swear words into the lens. Some of the words I've never heard before."

Estelle and Filomena laugh so hard that the rest of us follow suit. "You have to send us the links in the group chat. I can't wait to see them."

"The youngest, Chucky, yells into the camera, 'My grandpop has smelly ass socks that smell like a monkey's asshole!' Now, how they know what a monkey's a-hole smells like, I have no idea, but that made me chuckle."

"Remind me never to let you take off your shoes in public." Estelle pinches her nose in disgust.

Dennis taps the face of his watch. "I've got to get moving, folks. Keep a watchful eye out in the neighborhood. Report anything suspicious, and I'll tell you what I find out about Ziggy."

"Have you learned anything new about Adele and Vanessa Garrison?" I ask.

"After the coroner, I'm heading to the station. Let's meet in the morning for coffee and catch up on the case." Dennis picks up his pants, which are getting loose around his belly. The stress of these cases must be getting to him. I make a mental note to have Rebecca pick up some bagels for breakfast tomorrow.

"Where's Carol?" Bill looks past the dissipated crowd that has gathered since the ambulance left the property. There is no sign of her.

"She's been working long hours lately in the clinic. This flu season has been a doozy." Estelle takes her cell phone out of her tracksuit pocket. "I'll text her, make sure she's alright, and tell her about Ziggy if she doesn't already know and that we're meeting in the morning about the Garrison case."

I scurry quickly back home, eager to read the note left behind by Jeb.

My heart pounds, and the key fumbles in the lock. I rush into the bedroom, snatch the note from the nightstand, and settle into my armchair. I hold the note, savoring the moment. These little moments in life that bring joy need to be savored. I remind myself a lot these days. Wisdom is a gift. I take a deep breath and open the note.

My Dearest Diana,

Nearly sixty years, and somehow, last night felt like the first page of something new. I have cared for you in a thousand quiet ways over the years. Holding you close and waking up next to you felt like the most natural thing in the world. Last night was a delightful blur of laughter, warmth, and something I can't quite name. If you feel the same and don't want this to end here, if this is the next chapter of our lives, I would love to savor every word of it with you.

All my love,

Jeb

I kiss the note and hold it close to my heart. I recite in my head the conversation I'm sure will come with my daughter. Sorry, Lola, I know I promised no more male attachments . . . but this one . . . for once, you'll approve; he's for keeps.

Chapter Twenty-Three

Diana
Closing the Garrison Case

Dennis shows up this morning with a tray full of Mermaid Energy specialty drinks from The Googan Coffee Shop, made with lavender energy, huckleberry, and a gummy mermaid tail.

"Don't you sleep?" I ask. "You must have risen very early this morning to drive downtown."

"Not well. I get only about five to six hours of sleep each night. I mostly toss and turn, preoccupied with unresolved cases. I often wake up feeling restless around six a.m."

"Thank you for the morning pick-me-up," says Estelle.

"Is there any booze in this one?" asks Filomena.

Dennis rests his briefcase on his lap. "Nope. Get some coconut rum from the coffee station. We can spike our drinks with a little kick after I share what I uncovered about our case."

Filomena was up out of her chair, heading toward the coffee station for the rum before Dennis completed his sentence.

While Filomena is topping off our energy drinks with coconut joy, Jeb saunters toward us with a bag full of assorted bagels and cream cheeses from Max's Bagel Cafe. I can't suppress my smile. All eyes are on me. I'm burning up from the inside out, fully aware that everyone must know our little secret by now. No one mentions it. Jeb places the bagels on the table along with paper plates and napkins, rubs my back, and leaves us be.

Filomena sends a wink my way, and Estelle lifts her drink in my direction as a toast to a job well done of sorts. Bill scratches his scalp beneath his ever-growing man bun while Dennis is rifling through his briefcase for the morning paperwork and his current findings. Carol hasn't arrived yet.

"Let's eat first," I say to Dennis as he organizes his papers. "Carol isn't here yet, and I'm sure she'd like to hear about the case."

"Sure," he replies.

Moments later, we notice Carol and Tom engaged in a deep conversation at the back of the room.

"What is happening between those two?" Estelle mumbles.

"They've been spending a lot of time together these days," Filomena points out.

"Do you think there's something going on between them?" Estelle asks.

"He's a prick," Bill says under his breath.

"Exactly. A big one," Filomena clarifies, and we ladies laugh while the joke is lost among the men.

"I don't want to come across as the mean girl in the group, so please don't judge me too harshly for my comment. When a woman is dating a new man, she tends to dress nicely and make an effort to present herself well—smell better, at the very least. Lately Carol seems a bit . . . unwell and somewhat disheveled. Please don't hate me; I'm just making an observation."

"Is that why you smell so seductive today?" Bill asks with a smirk. "A new man in *your* life?" He waggles his eyebrows suggestively.

"Don't do that. It's disturbing," I tell him.

We divert our attention back to Carol and Tom. Carol turns her head and catches us gazing at them. She whispers something in Tom's ear before joining us at the table.

"What kind of potion are we drinking today?" she asks before settling down, steering the subject matter away from herself.

"Dennis picked up Mermaid Energy drinks at The Googan. We spiked them with a bit of coconut rum, and Diana's driver, Jeb, brought us a great selection from Max's Bagels. That's your recap," says Filomena. "What's happening between you and Tom? You two were talking so seriously."

"Nothing at all," Carol insists. "We were just chatting about some internal administrative matters . . . you know, boring inside baseball stuff."

"Hmm," Bill grumbles. "If you say so."

Carol grabs an everything bagel and takes a sip of her energy drink. "Yum. Tastes beachy. What's happening with the case?"

"Good news first or bad news?" Dennis lays his paperwork on the table.

"Bad news," we respond in unison.

"Bad news it is, then." Dennis shows us a letter from the FBI requesting the case takeover. "This is not a request; rather, it's more of a formality."

Some responses include:

"What?"

"That's bullpuckey!"

"Hogwash!"

"Mother flipper!"

"Begin at the start," I insist.

"In a nutshell," says Dennis, "we located Vanessa and her dog, Amos. As expected, she conveyed her belief that her stepmother was causing her illness. She rushed off to a wellness clinic and immediately began to feel better. She intended to confront her father about her sister's death and her illness, but hadn't mustered the courage to do so when we located her. From what I understand, the FBI has reason to believe that Adele's ex-husband may have died under suspicious circumstances."

"Sweet mother of Jesus! She killed her ex-husband too?" says Filomena.

"I wouldn't be surprised if both her ex-husband and her stepdaughter are exhumed." Bill lets out a big sigh of relief, then a smile. His pride shines through. You can see a sparkle in his eyes. He's thoroughly excited about this case's turn of events.

"I knew it! What an evil woman," Filomena says, fist-bumping her sister.

"Munchausen syndrome by proxy is an illness. No one is born evil; she must have experienced terrible childhood trauma," explains Carol.

"A mistreated and tormented childhood, perhaps, but murder? What kind of mother or stepmother would kill her own stepchildren and ex-husband?" Filomena banters back.

"Well, ex-husband . . . I can understand that," I joke. "Had I known her earlier, maybe I could have picked up a few pointers—just kidding, of course . . ." At least Bill laughs.

"Did they arrest her?" Bill asks.

"Yes. She was brought in for questioning regarding the allegations made by Vanessa, and there is an approved search warrant for her home and office. That's all I know." Dennis shows us the search warrant, then piles his papers and returns them to his briefcase.

"So is that the good news?" Carol asks.

"No. The good news is that we have successfully closed another cold case, and the Treasure Coast Cold Case Crimes Unit has awarded us four hundred dollars in gift cards to celebrate at the new Italian restaurant, Lynora's, in Palm City."

Chapter Twenty-Four

Diana
The Joy of Destroying Brain Cells

I used to love crime shows. I watched them all. Those sorts of stories used to delight me, relax me after a long day at the office. Now they settle in my stomach like curdled milk.

Strangely, I long for the days when my daughter, Lola, and I would curl up on the couch and watch *Real Housewives*, *Love Island*, or *Love is Blind*—something dumb and mindless. I would complain about watching those shows at the time. "Shut that off," I would say. "Those shows destroy brain cells." But, in all honesty, we would have so much fun watching the men admiring themselves in the mirror, and laughing at their 'roid rage when another man set their eye on the girl they wanted to shack up with.

I loved listening to Lola make fun of bird-brained twenty-something-year-old girls, with their fake tits and puppet lips trying to create drama where none existed just for ratings and Instagram followers—the good ol' days of television.

I can't watch those shows without her, but my secret addiction has always been *My 600-lb Life*. Don't tell anyone. There's something about watching a six-hundred-pound person complain that they're starving, working so hard, and dieting, after showing they ate six pancakes, a pack of bacon, and seven sausages for breakfast. It somehow makes me feel better about myself, sitting on the couch, allowing myself the joy of eating just four Nilla Wafers with my evening tea, which may or may not be spiked with a nip of Laird's 12 Year Old Apple Brandy. In my opinion, the best American-made apple brandy on the market is from America's oldest distillery. This habit, which I picked up from my grandfather, brings back fond memories.

Dr. Now is about to give a patient a "what for" when a text comes through from Jeb.

I've got a box of Nilla wafers and a bottle of champagne if you'd like to go on an adventure.

Chapter Twenty-Five

Theo

Ziggy's death was unexpected. I wish I hadn't had to end his life. But, just like the others, the world is better off without him. I tried minding my own business, but somehow, filth continues to find me.

Dear Reader,

April 2, 1984

There was a ten-year period when I didn't feel compelled to end anyone's life. Those were the good old days of working in the library. Eight blissful hours of work each day were primarily spent in silence. My evenings were devoted to pro bono legal work for a law firm known for advocating on behalf of prisoners they believed had been wrongly convicted. I've met only a few, but they do exist. It's the Lord's work and just as important as cleansing the streets of filth when I encounter it.

My ten-year stretch without a kill ended when I met Barbra. Barbra was a part-time traveling nurse and worked part-time at the library. We quickly became friends. You learn a lot about a person when you work together in a quiet place like a library, away from the usual noisy background chatter we call life. Outside of managing teenagers during after-school hours and returning borrowed books to their shelves, there's not much to do in the library except converse among ourselves.

Sometimes you can know too much about someone. This is a real phenomenon. One minute, you're best friends, and the next, they reveal something that can't be unsaid, and just like that, you despise them. That's it—like a light switch you turn off at bedtime. Done. Bye. Lights out. It's over.

I had long admired an emerald ring that Barbra wore. When I asked her about it, she led me to her locker in the employee lounge. She opened her backpack and emptied out a treasure trove of jewelry that would make any pirate jealous. "Take your pick," she said. When I inquired about how she acquired all this, she told me she had been working as a hospice nurse, and during the final stages of her patients' deaths, she looted them. That afternoon, I took the backpack from the locker room and dropped it off at the police station. That same evening, I pried open her bedroom window while she was asleep and did what I had to do.

Chapter Twenty-Six

Mr. Anderson

Watch, listen, learn. That's what I do best. Humans—what petty creatures they can be! They can sit on a bench in the park, surrounded by beauty, yet complain about a rat scurrying by their feet. Every creature has the right to enjoy a beautiful morning by the brook, even the ugly ones. Rats are among my favorite creatures. They're fun to chase and catch, and they're delicious. Yet humans loathe them simply because they're ugly. The fluffy-tailed ones, which humans call squirrels, are adored solely for their cuteness. I don't like them as much; they're harder to catch and not as tasty.

Humans are ruled by emotion, rarely in a good way. In my experience, most humans choose to hate passionately rather than love passionately. Many will say that love and hate are similar emotions, but they are not. Love is fleeting. Hate is far more passionate and far-reaching.

I often observe people sitting on the park bench, engaging in polite conversation about the lovely things they have in common. "Do you like birds?" one might ask. "I love birds," their companion would agree. "Oh, look at the cute squirrels!" they would both say. As soon as a rat scurries by, one or both will surely scream. "I hate rats," one would say, and the other would agree. That's when the genuine connection is made. People love to hate things together. You can almost feel the rage energy connection. Their hearts beat faster, their excitement hard to contain.

This morning my walk is abruptly halted when I find a lifeless Tom lying on the park bench by the brook. Before I get close enough to identify him, I smell that familiar scent of leather and waffles. A black bird pecks at one of his eyelids. I jump on top of the body to scare the bird away. Damn crows. They're the worst—no respect for the dead. It won't be long before the vultures come around.

I scurry off to Carol's house as fast as my furry feet will take me, meowing as profoundly and loudly as possible under her bedroom window.

"What is it, Mr. Anderson?" Carol asks after opening the window. I persist in berating her with more meows.

"Alright, let me put on my slippers. Hold on."

Within minutes, she follows me to Tom's bench. She doesn't seem surprised. She calls 911, speaks with dispatch, sends a text message, and when Dennis arrives, she picks me up and takes me back to her house.

"Okay, Mr. Anderson. You can stay with me while the police and firemen take care of Tom. I'm sorry you had to see that, but Tom was very sick. He was dying. I gave him some medicine to put him to sleep before he was in too much pain." She pets my head and then goes into the shower.

I roam around her house while she is preoccupied in the bathroom. I find a few needles in the kitchen and various medicine vials strewn across the island countertop. Did she help Tom kill himself? She doesn't feel bad about this? Why would humans do this to themselves? Shouldn't death be peaceful? I've witnessed lots of old folks slip away. It usually looks pretty peaceful. Why would Tom want to die on a park bench only to be pecked by crows and found like that by his friends? That doesn't make sense. I need to get back there to see if he has that same needle mark by his ear as Ziggy and Monty. Hurry up, Carol. Get dressed; we've got some investigating to do.

Chapter Twenty-Seven

Diana
Dinner with Jeb

I nestle into the front seat of the Bentley after a blissful welcoming kiss from Jeb. I fiddle with the air-conditioning vents to position them perfectly away from my eyes. My eyes tend to tear up when air blasts too vigorously in my direction. He's wearing the cologne I gifted him, and he smells delicious. I'd like to attack him right here, but I'm a lady, I remind myself, for crying out loud—a seventy-four-year-old one, no less. So, for the time being, I keep my hands to myself. I wonder if one ever outgrows being boy crazy. Maybe it's just me? Well, maybe it's just me and Blanche Devereaux from *The Golden Girls*. Sometimes I dream we're friends—two Southern gals with an obsession with beautiful, sexy men.

"This might be the first time I've ridden up front with you," I point out.

"I think you're right." He smirks. "How does it feel?"

"Unsafe."

"I think you meant to say adventurous."

"Yes. Right. That's exactly what I meant. So where are you taking me?"

"I thought we'd enjoy a lovely evening out at The Black Marlin in downtown Stuart. It's a bit too cool to sit outdoors, and The Black Marlin is one of my favorite hidden gems downtown that flies under the radar of snowbirds and vacationers. It's quaint and cozy, and the food is excellent."

"Sounds great," I say as my stomach rumbles loudly. "Sorry about that," I apologize. "It's been a busy day. I don't think I've eaten since breakfast. Tom was found dead this morning in the park. Natural causes, the paramedics say. I'm not so sure about that. Something about it doesn't sit right with me."

Jeb drums his fingers on the steering wheel. "Diana, I know you're excited about your newfound career in solving cold cases, and I'm happy that this has been occupying your time and helping with your transition into retirement. I love this for you. I also love that you're making friends. There was no way for you to build any *real* friendships in your old career."

"Right on there."

"But, tonight, can we just enjoy our own company without any doom, gloom, or devastating news about death?"

"Absolutely," I promise.

Jeb drops me off in front of the restaurant while he parks the car. Apparently, finding a parking spot downtown is akin to winning the lottery around here. Fortunately, I only have to wait a few minutes before Jeb shows up, his eyes bright with cheer. "The parking fairies granted my wish today."

He smiles as he opens the door for me to enter.

"Welcome, Mr. Donnelly," the hostess calls out.

"She recognized you straight away," I acknowledge. "Don't tell me you bring *all* your lady friends here?"

"I come here a few nights a week and sit at the bar alone. I'm sure they're excited that I have a beautiful woman to accompany me this evening."

"Flattery will get you everywhere," I say. Donnelly, I repeat in my mind. Diana Donnelly. I imagine I'm in high school, writing Diana Donnelly over and over again in cursive in my algebra notebook to pass the time. Even in my seventies, when lovestruck, I revert back to my teenage silliness. I wonder why that is. I guess we only really age on the outside.

Before the waitress even introduces herself, she arrives at our booth holding a bottle of Crémant de Bourgogne sparkling wine and two flutes.

"It's not the fanciest champagne," Jeb apologizes, "but it is surprisingly tasty."

His hazel-green eyes sparkle. The ladies are on point; he does indeed look alarmingly like an older, more dapper, gentlemanly version of Jason Momoa. A beast of a man. My own personal Aquaman. Forget Diana Donnelly; how about Sugar Momoa? I love this for me.

I raise my champagne flute for a toast. "To us. To forever together." It's bold, I know, but I'm brave.

He smiles. I never realized how perfectly aligned all of his teeth are. Nothing is more attractive than a man who cares for his teeth.

We clink and sip. "Yes. This is surprisingly good," I admit.

I choose the pistachio-crusted black grouper, while he selects the signature black marlin meatloaf, which he assures me never disappoints.

Dinner is delightful, and Jeb is easy to talk to. I often catch myself smiling during dinner to the point that my cheeks are starting to feel sore.

"Lola and Lydia are coming to visit soon. Would you like to spend time with us when they get here?"

Jeb looks puzzled.

"I mean, not driving us around, but enjoying the weekend with us, you know . . . without all the driving. As a matter of fact, maybe I'll ask Rebecca to take us about town."

"Egad! Not Rebecca. Have you seen the way that woman drives?"

"Well, no."

"Good for you. She's a hot mess with a bad temper. She's got a heavy foot, and she loves to play the horn and shout with her middle finger."

"Oh my!"

"Lovely girl. But dear God! She's a menace behind the wheel."

"I will make other arrangements then," I say.

He reaches over and squeezes my hand from across the table. "I look forward to it."

For the first time in a long time, I feel happy. It's like the warm and fuzzy feeling you get during the kissing scene of a rom-com when the unlikely couple finally gets together. I'm self-aware enough to know that my troubles with men are a problem with me. I pick the wrong men on purpose. Not this time. I deserve better. I deserve Aquaman. This one is for keeps.

On the walk back to the car, we decide to stroll along the boardwalk to enjoy a brisk walk and the glowing moonlight over the Intracoastal, when a group text comes through.

Meet in the morning. A new cold case.

Chapter Twenty-Eight

Diana
A Very Old Cold Case

I wake up sore. A seventy-four-year-old body is not meant to contort in the ways it did last night. I reach over to his side of the bed, and, like the last time he stayed over, it's empty. What time does this man wake up in the morning? I hear him rummaging around in the kitchen: cling, clang, sizzle. Then I smell it—the greatest scent planet Earth has to offer: bacon.

"A great lover and a chef? How did I get so lucky?" I say, walking toward him in the kitchen. This giant man wielding a tiny spatula looks entirely out of place in my small kitchen.

"Thank you for the compliments, but you haven't tasted my breakfast yet," he says, handing me a cup of coffee as I sit down at the kitchen island to watch him finish cooking.

"In comparison to my own cooking, it will be Michelin level," I promise.

While he's cooking, I open the Facebook app on my phone to see what's stirring up among Jensen

Beach locals, because who doesn't love a little melodrama with their breakfast? Maybe it's a retiree thing.

I read the local headlines out loud to Jeb as he cooks. "Someone is looking for a good Chinese food restaurant—boring." Okay, what else? I scroll down further. "Oh, there is a video of a loggerhead turtle returning to sea after depositing her precious eggs onshore. Adorable." This makes my heart melt. I love sea turtle season. "There are a few posted videos of SpaceX rocket launches. There seems to be one every week these days. The new Costco opens on April twenty-fifth, but the gas station is open, and the gas price today is two eighty-five. Woo-hoo! People are very excited. No drama yet," I say, and continue to scroll. "Our local photographers, Steve Shive and Jim Ferro, have posted beautiful sunset photos. Finally, someone is reporting an accident at the roundabout at Confusion Circle in downtown Stuart. People are complaining that snowbirds shouldn't drive, and someone is saying if you can't see *over* the wheel, you shouldn't be able to *take* the wheel. Someone else wrote Don't tread on me . . . Yankees, go home!"

Jeb serves two slices of French toast and two slices of bacon, then sits beside me at the kitchen island counter. "So you have a new cold case today?"

"Yes, we'll meet at the country club in about an hour."

"Am I driving you somewhere today?"

"I'm not sure. I hope Dennis doesn't take us on that dreadful short bus. It smelled like a dumpster truck filled with circus animals. I'll let you know. Are you free today? Or do you have any plans of your own?"

"I was thinking that, since you'll be busy with your new cold case, I'll drive up to Jacksonville to visit my son, Simon, and his wife, Cheryl. He doesn't have any heart surgeries planned in the next few days, and it's been a while since I've seen them."

"That's a great idea. Please send my love, will you? It's been quite a while since I last saw them. Their kids must be in college by now, right?"

"Yes, one is attending the University of Miami as a pre-med student, while the other wants to be a journalist and has chosen Brown University in Rhode Island."

"You must really be proud."

"I am. Perhaps next time you'll join me for a visit?"

"I'd love to," I say, kissing him on the cheek before reaching for more maple syrup.

"That's a lot of syrup," he scolds as I drench my French toast with it. "That's too much sugar; you're going to get diabetes."

"I'm seventy-four . . . I'm going to eat it all. Everything. I'm happy to have come this far in life. Whatever comes next . . . bring it on."

"Okay, Diana . . . my sugar queen," he says, using air quotes with his fingers.

"That's very funny! Technically Lola is the reigning sugar queen, so I suppose that makes me the queen mother."

"So that would make me a sugar mother fu—"

I kiss him before he can finish his statement. Some things are better left unsaid.

By the time I arrive at the country club, everyone has already arrived. All eyes are on me as I prance over to the table. "Am I late?"

"No, we just got an early start," Filomena says, bubbling with excitement.

"No coffee today?" I inquire.

"Carol is making it." Bill gestures toward the coffee station. Creamer is spilling over the edge of the counter, and paper towels are scattered across the floor. The high-pitched whir of the blender leaves us all wondering what she's whipping up over there.

"She's making a huge mess." I point out the obvious.

Estelle and Dennis turn to look, shake their heads, and shrug.

Bill stands up to help Carol carry the mugs to the table.

"What are we drinking today?" Filomena asks, clapping her hands together.

"Today we're having a mudslide. It has a bit more booze than coffee and is a little heavy on the ice cream, but I'm sure you'll love it. It features vodka, Baileys, Kahlúa, vanilla ice cream, chocolate syrup, and just a splash of coffee."

She and Bill place the coffee mugs on the table. I swear, these coffee mugs are the best part of the day.

Carol thinks carefully and hands them out one at a time. She gives a mug to Filomena that reads "It's weird being the same age as old people." Then she hands another to Bill that says "I never dreamed I'd be a grumpy old man, yet here I am killing it." Estelle's mug features a unicorn jumping over a rainbow.

"That's my favorite one," Estelle cheers.

"I snatched it from Fat Harriett's grubby hands, so . . . you're welcome." Carol nods to Estelle.

"Fat Harriett? How fat is she?" Bill eggs Carol on.

"Hush up, she's sitting right behind you," warns Filomena.

Carol takes the bait and says, "She's so fat that when she was interviewed on Channel Six, you could see her sides on Channels Five and Seven." We all laugh. Then Carol adds, "One more . . . she's so fat she uses Google Earth to take a selfie."

I inadvertently glance over at Harriett. I feel terrible, but she shows no sign of having noticed the nonsense happening at our table at her expense.

Filomena plugs her ears. "God is going to strike us down at any moment. Those jokes are terrible. That poor woman. It's simply not right to mock the morbidly obese."

"You're right, sister. No more jokes." Estelle smacks Bill on the arm.

"What are you smacking *me* for?" Bill complains.

"You started it. Bad Bill." Estelle smacks him again.

Carol explains, "Don't be mad at me. She calls *herself* Fat Harriett."

"Holy moly! There's no way that could be true." I shake my head in disdain.

"Yes, she introduces herself that way," Carol says confidently.

"No. She's German." Filomena jumps in to clarify. "She introduces herself as Frau Harriett, not Fat Harriett—it might be time for a hearing aid, Carol."

Carol's face turns three shades of red. "Alright. Boozy coffee time." She pushes a mug toward Dennis that reads "I hate everyone equally." She keeps one for herself, adorned with hypodermic needle artwork that says "I'm the office prick." Then she slides a mug toward me that states "All I ask is that you treat me no differently than you would the Queen." I love this mug, but I'm not sure if I'm supposed to. Should I be offended? Part of me wants to comment on it, while another part wants to steal it and bring it home with me to cherish it.

"Are these new?" asks Bill.

"Yes. I went thrifting this past weekend in Mount Dora and came back with ten new mugs. I bought all of the mugs in the country club. You would think I'd get a little respect. I don't. These folks are a bunch of thieves. I've bought over a hundred and fifty mugs in the past five years, but there were fewer than forty this morning."

"Well, they're hilarious. People love them. It's a compliment, Carol," Filomena says, rubbing Carol's back. "People around here adore you and your mugs.

It's a joy to wake up in the morning, grab a cup of coffee, and read the new sayings on the mugs."

"We must embrace all the small joys in life," Estelle replies, smiling. "Everyone talks about how traveling back in time and doing something small can drastically change the present, but no one ever talks about how doing something small *today* can drastically change the future."

"I doubt a coffee mug is going to cure cancer or end the war in the Middle East," Bill says sarcastically.

Estelle smacks Bill's arm. "You know what I meant. Don't be a jackass."

"No swearing," Bill reminds Estelle.

"Not a swear word. It's an animal—*you're* an animal."

"Enough of all that hooey! How's my drink?" asks Carol.

Responses from the group include, "Delicious," "Tasty," "Boozy," and "Oh my, I'm not driving this morning."

Dennis sets his briefcase on his lap, pulls out a file, and places it on the table.

Bill slaps the table with both hands, creating a drumroll. "Drumroll, please," he urges, encouraging Dennis to open our new case officially.

"This case is an old one. A very old one. We're going back to 1968 for this one. Mabel Gladstone was stabbed in her home and left for dead while her two small children were at school. The last people to see her alive were the milkman and her neighbor Jill at approximately ten-thirty a.m. on the morning of February second, 1968."

"What about the knife?" Bill inquires.

"It was left behind. Although the DNA evidence is degraded, forensics is doing its best. I thought we'd take a drive out to the house tomorrow."

"Yay! Another field trip," cheers Estelle.

"Hey, before we go any further, can we discuss Tom?" Carol asks.

"Sure," Dennis agrees. "Tom was found on a bench by the creek, and his death was ruled as natural causes. He fell asleep on the bench and never woke up. His medical records indicated that he had recently been diagnosed with pancreatic cancer, so he was fortunate to have passed away peacefully."

"Was there an autopsy?" Carol taps her fingers on the table and shifts in her seat.

"No. His family didn't ask for one, the county wouldn't pay for one, and all indications suggest natural causes."

"Well, I don't believe Tom's death was natural. Yes, he had cancer, and it was stage four. He knew his days were numbered, but I'm telling you, something about his death doesn't feel right. He and I had grown fairly close over the past few weeks. I know . . . well, I'm certain that his death was no accident."

"Yeah, we noticed all the whispering and late-night greetings." Bill raises his eyebrows suggestively.

"Stop that. You look like a pervert when you do that. I was meeting him to give him pain medication to ease his suffering," Carol explains.

"Oh, that makes sense, I guess." Bill backs down.

Carol adds, "He told me that someone was stalking him."

"Stalking him?" I perk up. "Now this is getting interesting."

"One night he even caught someone in his bedroom peering over his bed. However, he pulled a revolver out from under his pillow, and the person ran off." Carol gestures, shooting us with her fingers.

"Person? Man or woman?" asks Estelle.

"He didn't say."

"That's so strange. This neighborhood is really safe," says Filomena.

"Exactly. That's why he thought someone in our community was out to get him." Carol's eyes widen as she glances at each of us for approval.

"Why would anyone be out to get Tom?" I ask.

"I'm not exactly sure, but I'm determined to find out. His daughter is coming tomorrow to collect his belongings, and I will meet with her to see if I can learn more about Tom before he lived and worked here."

"You probably won't be much help on the cold case tomorrow, Carol, since it's so old and there were no pets involved. Let us know what you find out about Tom," Dennis says, closing the case file and putting it back in his briefcase.

"I'm sorry for your loss," I say. "I understand how much Tom meant to you."

Estelle and Filomena reach across the table to hold Carol's hand, and I lay my hand on top of theirs.

"He will be missed," says Estelle.

"Yes, he will," Filomena agrees.

"To Tom," I say, lifting my mug. Everyone follows suit. The girls smile while Bill and Dennis exchange eye rolls as we clink our mugs and sip. "To Tomfoolery. May you rest in peace."

Thunder rumbles in the distance. A moment later, a clap of thunder. The chandelier above us sways back and forth, and the floor beneath us trembles. The lights flicker off and on twice.

"Geez Louise, that's God's wrath . . . because you made fun of Harriett. We're all going to hell in a hand-basket," Filomena scolds Carol.

"Maybe it's Tom making a toast with us from the other side," I suggest in jest.

Estelle puts both her hands on the table, feeling it vibrate. "It's a sign from Tom, alright. He's telling us that we need to look further into his death. I'm sure of it."

Chapter Twenty-Nine

Diana
Who Killed Mabel?

One of the greatest joys of winter in South Florida is leaving the windows open and welcoming nature's music inside. This morning I woke up to the Florida East Coast Railway chugging along with a few toots, soon followed by the controversial Brightline super-fast commuter train that might run you down and send you off to an early grave if you don't get off the tracks in time. Pay attention . . . don't lollygag around the railroad tracks, or you'll end up six feet under in no time.

Cardinals sing and enjoy their breakfast at the feeder. I reach over to Jeb's side of the bed. It's empty, as I expect it to be. I know he's visiting his son and daughter-in-law. For just a moment, I pretend he's up making breakfast for me, which brings me a smile. I already miss him. I can't spend time in my fantasyland this morning, however. There's work to be done—a new cold case.

I sit up in bed and pull my feet over the side. My right ankle is slightly swollen. It swells up sometimes.

It doesn't hurt. I can hear my doctor's voice in my head right now. Diana, you need to drink more water and eat less sugar. Blah, blah, blah, Doctor Some-Name-I-Can't-Remember, with two first names like Dr. John James or Dr. James John. Who cares? I'll worry about my ankle another day. I climb out of bed, shower, put on jeans and a sweater, down a quick cup of joe, and out the door I go.

The sleek black minibus looks brand new. Estelle, Filomena, and Dennis are waiting for my arrival. I check my Apple Watch and see that I'm five minutes early.

"Why do I always feel like I'm late?" I ask out loud to no one in particular.

"Don't mind us," Filomena says. "Estelle and I are early risers and always excited for a new case."

"You're right on time." Dennis nods toward the driver as he opens the hydraulic doors for us.

"Where's Bill?" I ask.

"He stayed back with Carol to meet Tom's daughter. Carol is quite sure there must be foul play regarding Tom's death, but I couldn't find any clues suggesting that could be true." Dennis extends his arm, allowing me to climb the steps onto the bus in front of him.

Once we are settled on the bus, I remark, "This bus smells much better than the last one. It smells like leather."

"Yes, ma'am. It's brand new." Dennis smiles at me.

"Traveling with the sugar queen has its perks," jokes Filomena. "We get such nice things."

"Happy to set the bar high." I smile back at Dennis.

"So tell us what to expect today," says Estelle.

"We've got a ten-minute ride into the town of Rio."

"Is it near Mrs. Peters Smokehouse? Can we stop for some fish dip before we head back?" Estelle asks. "Their Wahoo smoked dip is the best!"

"Sure," Dennis says.

The bus arrives at a small white house with a red door on Northeast Banyan Drive.

"This is where Mabel lived." Dennis reads the real estate listing from Zillow. "It's a timeless, quiet refuge that looks like a home time left behind. The small two-bedroom house has one and a half baths, measures approximately eight hundred and fifty square feet, and features a metal roof. It's an old, cozy Florida home built in 1957."

Filomena adds, "This house is old but charming. It could use a little help with landscaping. It has only two palm trees and a few hedges, but no flowers. This home needs some color."

"A red door . . . could be a bad omen," Estelle mutters.

"Not necessarily. Do you know what a red door signifies?" I ask.

"No. What?" asks Estelle.

"In America, it means people are welcome at the homes that host a red door. During the Civil War and the days of the Underground Railroad, runaway slaves would see a red door as a safe house and potential escape to the railroad tunnels. In Scotland, a red door means that your mortgage is paid off. In Ireland, a red door is thought to ward off ghosts or evil spirits. In Florida, it's a symbol of hospitality."

"So interesting," says Estelle.

"Maybe Mabel is haunting this house?" wonders Filomena out loud.

Dennis tells the young lady driver to pick us up in half an hour.

"Do we have permission to be here?" I ask.

"Yes, the homeowner knows we will be looking around the property, although we're not allowed inside," Dennis explains.

"Can we peek through the windows?" I ask.

Dennis rubs his bald head. "Probably not, but I'll look the other way if you do."

Estelle and Filomena sit side by side on the steps where Mabel was stabbed in 1968. Filomena pulls her tarot cards out of a small wooden box while Estelle sits quietly on the stoop.

Dennis and I walk around to the backyard.

"How exactly can I help?"

Dennis suggests, "Since the DNA evidence is degraded, as I explained, I've been informed that there's a lab in Central Florida with brand-new equipment that may be helpful to us. The challenge I've encountered is the age of this case, coupled with limited funding and the absence of family members advocating to get the case closed. I was hoping you could persuade one of our local state representatives to make a call to our office to get this approved."

"So why did you take on this case? The murderer is most likely dead, anyway," I suggest.

"The new homeowner is the president of the Jensen Beach Women's Association. Apparently she's pissed off that the Realtor didn't tell her that someone was murdered in this house."

"Don't you have to disclose that information?"

"Florida has no requirement for disclosure of death on a property," he says flatly. "Suicide, natural death, or homicide. Florida statute 689.25."

"That's not right." I shake my head.

"Agreed. Nevertheless, the homeowner is angry about this and demanded that we try to close this case."

"Why? Is this place haunted or something?" I wonder.

"Who knows? That's not something people discuss outside our small circle. I'm sure if she brought it up, others would think she's a nut."

"Absolutely. I'll make a few phone calls," I promise. "I'm confident I can get one of my political acquaintances to reach out and secure approval for this funding."

"Thank you!"

By the time Estelle and Filomena meet up with us, they seem pretty cheery.

"Well, how did it go?" I ask.

"I'll put it all in writing. But I'm going to tell you that she knew her killer, and it was a woman," Filomena says with confidence.

"I'll second that," says Estelle.

"Holy honey bees!" I say, still unable to swear since I've been training myself not to. "A woman? This is our third case where a woman is the killer. What is the world coming to?"

"Female killers are quite rare. So, yes. If this is true, it would be a remarkable coincidence," Dennis adds. "Alright, let's regroup soon. Please record your findings on paper. In the meantime, Diana will try to get funding approved for the expensive DNA testing on the knife."

As we hop back onto the bus, Dennis suggests that we stop at Mrs. Peters Smokehouse. Afterward, we head to the newly opened restaurant in Rio, The Weedline Grill, for some fresh conch salad and fish sandwiches.

"How fun! Our own little bus tour and taste of Rio," Filomena cheers. "Carol and Bill will be jealous they missed out on all the fun. The best part of these bus tours has been the food excursions!"

Up to now, retirement has revolved around themed parties, anytime cocktails, and food. I must say . . . it's not terrible.

Chapter Thirty

Theo

In 1985, I embarked on a new career, leaving education, books, and higher learning behind. I set out to flush out the bad guys and potentially apply my investigative talents to catch some of these criminals before they could cause further harm.

I was hired as an investigative journalist at the *Miami Herald* in the spring of 1985, a job I loved. I love puzzles, and I love to dig deep into a mystery and try to solve it. The assignments are even more rewarding if what I uncover is for the greater good.

My assignments primarily involved money laundering, drug trafficking, kidnapping, and attempted murder, and my days were never dull. When the cases became controversial and the details I wrote seemed too risky to disclose, my editor allowed the articles to be credited simply as Staff Writer.

Over the years, I covered notable events such as the 1985 Miami River Cops Scandal, the 1986 FBI Miami shootout, and the 1989 Miami riot in Overtown, among others.

Dear reader,

Dec 2, 1991

*At this point in my story, you might think that I'm a monster. I want to assure you that **monsters—true monsters—run in packs**. Highlight this. Underline it. It's a central theme of humanity. One person can cause only so much harm, but an institution—a pack of wolves, so to speak—that, my friend, can be catastrophic. Some say there is a fine line between cop and criminal. In my opinion, it's an invisible line that's difficult to trace.*

What drives their personalities may be the same; they simply choose different roles to express them. Doesn't this apply to all of humanity? Aren't we all fundamentally equal parts good and evil? Evil is a harsh word. Bad is too vague. Sinful—better. It must be sinful, because God forgives sins. That's what we're told, anyway. Evil cannot be forgiven. Choices. Life is full of them. Choices guide our paths in life. Choose wisely.

Federal DEA agents seized 23,641 pounds of cocaine at the port of Miami. Over two weeks, thirty-eight cocaine cowboys were arrested. The country cheered. However, what you might not know is that seven deceased police informants rest at the bottom of the Miami River. I covered the story but didn't disclose the casualties and secrets rotting below—secrets these men could reveal about corrupt cops on the take.

The eighth body, lying alongside the seven, is a DEA agent who fell shortly after the drug bust. This particular agent was on the verge of receiving all the glory for the arrests. Luckily, I stepped in to correct that injustice, as he was, in fact, their inside man all along—until he wasn't. He was supplying information to the drug cartel about what the DEA knew regarding their organization.

He probably would have slithered out of this mess somehow had I not stepped in to correct this situation. Honor culture runs rampant in these circles. Some monsters shouldn't be protected. We need to learn this as a species. Nevertheless, I awarded myself with a stockpile of money I found hidden in his bedroom closet ceiling (stupid hiding spot). He now resides with the fishes, where he belongs.

Chapter Thirty-One

Mr. Anderson

The deaths of Monty, Ziggy, and Tom are related. I'm one hundred percent sure.

When I found them, they all had the same needle prick behind their ear. No one noticed this essential detail other than me. Sadly, because they were old and ill, autopsies were never completed. I'm not sure why someone is killing off the retirees at Ocean's Edge, but I'm determined to get to the bottom of this.

Today Carol and Bill visit Tom's townhouse with his daughter. I prance inside behind Bill, leap onto the couch, and listen intently to their conversation and all the niceties, small talk, and silly gibberish that humans spew before getting down to important topics.

It's still cool outside, and the windows are open. The neighbors are new to the neighborhood and younger—in their late fifties. They're blasting Lady Gaga's latest song, "Abracadabra." I love this song, so I dance along and wag my tail to the music.

Tom's daughter has long red hair and green eyes. She appears guarded and overly reserved, suggesting she has experienced past injuries, whether physical or emotional.

Typically people stand twelve to eighteen inches apart, but she prefers more personal space. She paces backward whenever Bill gets too close. She fears older men and doesn't trust Carol. She turns away when Carol attempts to shake her hand. She guides Bill and Carol to the kitchen table and brings them each a glass of water. She sits, looking annoyed, with her expression suggesting she'd rather be anywhere else but here.

"There's nothing I'd like to keep here," the redhead says. "Do you know of a place I can call that will haul away unwanted items for charity?"

"Sure. I can make a few suggestions," Carol offers. "You'll have to box up the smaller items on your own, though."

"I can do that," the redhead says with a nod.

"The reason Bill and I are meeting you today, however, is not to discuss Tom's belongings but rather to inquire whether he had any enemies who might have wished him harm?"

"Enemies? Where are you going with this? He had stage four cancer. He was not well. Why would anyone harm a dying man?"

"Well, we were hoping you could help answer that question."

"Hold on. The police said that he died of natural causes. Is that not the case?"

"Technically, yes, on paper. However, I wanted to meet with you to explore whether, for some strange reason, he did not die of natural causes. What might be another reason? Do you know of anyone who might want to harm your dad?"

"No. He was, however, a ladies' man. He had affairs with several women, but those are long in the past. Most of those women have passed away. No one hated my dad. He tried to be friendly with everyone." The redhead shrugs and lets out an exasperated sigh. "Didn't you work with him here at The Ocean's Edge, Carol? You know he's friendly and gets along with everyone. Why would anyone want to harm him?"

"Are you his only daughter?" Carol asks.

"As far as I know, there are no other children."

"Were you close?" Bill asks.

The redhead narrows her eyes at Bill. She really does not like him. She shifts her gaze to his man bun and distorts her face, which clearly conveys *yuck* without needing to say it. "Why all the questions? I promise you I did not kill my dad. We were close. I loved my dad. Do you have any other questions before I start packing up his belongings?"

"No. Thank you for meeting with us," Carol says, her shoulders slumped and looking defeated.

"Take the cat with you. I'm allergic."

"Come on, Mr. Anderson. Let's go." Carol shoos me off the couch.

"Did you say Mr. Anderson?"

"Yes. That's the cat's name. Why?"

"Well, my dad used to talk about Mr. Anderson. He mentioned something to me the last time we spoke. It was something like . . . only Mr. Anderson knows what's really happening around here."

I perk up. Finally I have some attention! I glare at Carol and say, "Follow me." Everyone else hears "Meow." Carol understands my language. I scurry into Tom's bedroom, with Carol, Bill, and the redhead trailing behind. I jump up on Tom's desk by the bedroom window. I often leaped into his window in the evening, and he'd let me sit on his desk while he worked. Mostly tedious paperwork for the sales office, but he was also working on an intriguing theory about some recent deaths at The Ocean's Edge.

"Okay, Mr. Anderson, what are you trying to tell us?" asks Carol.

I pat my right paw on the desk drawer three times and stare at Carol. She knows what this means. Carol opens the drawer and rifles through the files inside. When she finds the right file, I say, "That's it." The humans hear another "Meow." The file is titled *Murder at The Ocean's Edge?*

Carol opens the file to discover a list of names and deaths dating back four years. Included on the list are both Monty and Ziggy. Beside each name is a crime. Next to Monty's name, the crime listed is money laundering, and for Ziggy, it's child pornography.

"I am not entirely sure what I'm looking at here." Carol's face heats up, and droplets of sweat bead along her jawline and neck. She's angry.

Bill leans over her shoulder to read along with her. "We need to send this file to Dennis as soon as possible."

"Who's Dennis?" the redhead asks.

"Retired detective. He lives here."

"What does any of this have to do with my father's death? I'm not connecting the dots here. Help me."

"I don't have any answers for you right now," Carol explains. "Yes, your dad had stage four cancer. Yes, he was going to pass away soon. However, I think he stumbled across some information that may have led him to an early grave."

"What information?"

"I'm not sure yet. It's speculation. Folks have been dying here, natural causes, so they say, but Tom thought otherwise. He believed folks were being killed off because of their past crimes."

"What? We never talked about this, Carol." Bill looks perplexed. "You never mentioned anything about this."

"It was a stupid conspiracy theory Tom had that maybe some folks were being offed for their past crimes. I told him it couldn't be, yet here we are with a list of names dating back years of people who lived here, who died by natural causes, listing their crimes beside their names."

"All this? Right under our noses?" Bill scratches his head and glares at me. "Did you know about this all along, Mr. Anderson? What other secrets can you tell?"

I wag my tail in a circle. This means I have a lot to say.

"So . . . what was my dad's crime?"

"I think he knew too much. I think he knew who the killer was. I think the killer lives here among us," Carol surmises.

I jump off the desk. There is nothing more satisfying than being heard.

"Mr. Anderson, I'll have a special slice of Key lime pie ready just for you tonight after dinner," Carol promises.

Scratch that. There is nothing better than being heard *and* appreciated.

Chapter Thirty-Two

Diana
My 75th Birthday

For my daughter and granddaughter's visit, I chose a beautiful pink midi dress with two-inch cream-colored wedge sandals. I stood in front of the full-length mirror and told myself, Not bad for seventy-five.

My front door drifts open, and little Lydia rushes through it to give me a big, warm hug. Oh, how I love this little minion! She's the spitting image of me at her age and just as feisty. I adore a feisty child; rarely do well-behaved women leave an indelible mark upon the world!

Lola hands me a shiny silver gift bag and pink roses, which are my favorite.

Lydia sings "Happy Birthday" while spinning in circles, making her dress twirl and swirl around her.

Jeb follows Lola through the front door, holding a bottle of Perrier Jouet Champagne. "Seventy-five," he says, kissing my cheek. "That's a milestone."

"Every year without a tombstone is a milestone," I joke.

"Open your gift," Lola suggests. "You're going to love it."

"Where's your hubby today?" I ask while tearing apart the gift wrap.

"Working. Always working." I can see the sadness on her face, and I can easily recall and empathize with the days of raising her with the hectic work schedules her dad and I once had.

Lola and Lydia are dressed identically in matching black cocktail dresses with white lace embroidery on the sleeves. Lydia's black patent leather Mary Jane shoes match Lola's black patent leather stilettos. I give her credit for still being able to wear such high heels. I had to give those up years ago.

"You ladies look lovely today. Stunning. What beauties you two are." I compliment my girls. I understand the importance of a compliment from a parent, especially from moms to daughters. We are shaped by the people we love.

Jeb takes the flowers from my hands and begins to snip the stems for placement in a vase while I open Lola's gift.

A stunning red Valentino box encases a beautiful shoulder bag adorned with dazzling silver crystals, so blingy that I couldn't possibly get lost in a crowd. "This is spectacular."

"I thought you'd love it. I heard through the grapevine that there's a disco party here soon. This will be a great accessory."

"Yes. But this must have cost a fortune. You didn't need to—"

She cuts me off. "You deserve nice things, Mom. Plus, I'm the sugar queen now . . . I can afford it."

I hug her while Lydia clings to my legs to avoid feeling left out.

"Through what grapevine did you hear about a disco dance party? I didn't even know about that one."

"I read about it on the website's activity page," Lola explains.

"Oh, I guess I've been a bit preoccupied lately," I say, feeling myself blush as I glance over toward Jeb.

Jeb is busy filling the vase with water. He places the roses in the vase and finds a spot for them on the kitchen island. He retrieves three flutes from the cabinet and pours champagne for a toast. "Happy seventy-five, and more to come." He pauses for a moment, takes a deep breath, and says, "We love you." Jeb's eyes tear up as he clinks our glasses.

Lola's eyes dart back and forth from me to Jeb.

"How did I not see this coming? You two are in love?" She looks dumbfounded.

"Am I going to have a new grandpa?" Lydia asks. "Grandpa Jeb, Grandpa Jeb," she chants.

"Maybe," says Jeb, looking at my reaction for approval.

"Alright. This is too much for me. I'm seventy-five. Y'all are going to give me a heart attack," I say, clutching my heart.

Jeb reaches into his pocket and pulls out a tiny blue box.

Oh no. Seriously? I'm burning up inside. I did not see this coming at all.

"Seriously?" I open the box to reveal what looks like an emerald-cut, four-carat diamond ring.

Jeb says, "I'm too old to drop to one knee. I might not be able to get back up. I've waited almost sixty years for this moment. Would you do me the honor of becoming Diana Donnelly, the role you were always meant for?"

"Yes, I will," I say without even considering the words spilling from my mouth. Of course I will. The silly fictional scribblings in my algebra book come flooding back to me like I somehow wished this into existence.

After a very long kiss, we're interrupted by Lydia's smoochy noises and Lola's "Hello, there are other people in the room here, you know."

"I'm hungry. Can we eat now?" asks Lydia.

"Yes. The limo is waiting for us," Jeb says.

"Limo. Yay! I love limos." Lydia twirls around again in delight.

"Where are we going?"

"Kyle G's on the water on Hutchinson Island for an exquisite and memorable seventy-fifth birthday for you and our lovely little family." Jeb hoists Lydia into his arms, kisses her on the cheek, then sets her back down.

Lydia smiles because she enjoys the attention. She hugs Jeb but quickly wipes his kiss off her cheek. "Yuck. Kisses are gross."

Jeb retrieves another ring from his pocket. It's a candy ring. "This one is for you," he says. He hands the ring to Lydia, who immediately tears open the plastic wrapper, licks the ring, and places it on her finger.

"Look, Grandma, just like you." She beams.

"We're going to have to hire a new driver," I point out.

"Indeed," Jeb agrees.

Before we head out, a group text comes through.

Meet tomorrow 5 p.m. at the country club. Minibus will take us to dinner at Lynora's to recap the Mabel

I read the text. I decide not to respond. I place my phone on the kitchen island. I'm going to leave it at home and spend the day giving my full attention to my family and fiancé.

I stare down at my engagement ring and glance lovingly at Jeb, Lola, and Lydia. I'm very thankful to have these people in my life. I lock the door to my townhouse as we make our way to the limo. My seventy-fifth birthday is shaping up to be the best day ever.

Chapter Thirty-Three

Diana
Recapping the Mabel Case

Before heading out to catch the murder minivan for dinner, I grab the leather satchel, hidden in the kitchen cabinet, that I discovered by the brook, full of syringes and vials of strange, toxic medicine. I toss it into my oversized purse. I had almost completely forgotten about finding this. The night of the Rednecks and Renegades dance was a blur, and I was definitely drunk, but it's funny how easily some things slip your mind at my age. I've been meaning to hand the satchel over to Dennis, but so much has been happening lately. Anyway, there's no time like the present.

As usual, I'm not late, but still last to arrive and greet the others. Estelle is the first to notice the new bling on my left hand.

"You tussle around with Jason Momoa a few times and now you're engaged? What kind of secret enchantment do you bestow to mesmerize all your men? I want some!" Estelle grabs my left hand for a closer look.

Filomena peeks over her shoulder. "Wow, that sure is impressive. Does he have a few single brothers for us?"

"What is this? Engagement number ten?" Bill grumbles quietly.

"I heard that. Don't be so dramatic. It's not been near that many. Be happy for me, Bill."

"Don't get your sugar britches in a twist! I *am* happy for you. But you might be a serial wife—"

I cut him off. "Maybe. I'm aware of my shortcomings, Bill. I don't need you to point them out. This time, though, I think this marriage will stick. We've known each other for, I don't know, close to sixty years. We're best friends. Be nice. Pretend to be happy for me."

"We are all happy for you. Bill is a pooper." Estelle smacks Bill in the arm.

"Ouch," Bill yelps.

"Be nice, or we won't be taking you out on field trips anymore. We'll leave you behind to hang out with Fat Harriet," Carol chimes in.

"Frau Harriett," Filomena corrects her.

"Sure." Carol rolls her eyes. Frau, fat, same thing.

Dennis gestures to the driver to open the doors, and we pile on board.

"Congratulations," Dennis says when we're seated.

"I'm happy for you," Carol adds.

I open my purse and hand the leather satchel to Dennis. "I found this by the brook the night of the Rednecks and Renegades dance."

Dennis's eyes grow wide. He opens the leather satchel and rummages through its contents but says nothing.

"What's in there?" Bill peeks inside.

Carol snatches the satchel from Dennis and pulls out a vial of propofol and another vial of fentanyl. "This shit can kill you. Where exactly did you find this?"

"In plain sight, by the brook on the path back to my townhouse," I explain.

"Why did you hold onto this for so long?" asks Bill. "Why didn't you tell us about this sooner?"

"Good question. At first, I didn't think much of it. I assumed it might be someone's personal stash. I nearly left it by the brook, but something urged me to keep it. Anyway, I brought it home, shoved it in a kitchen cabinet, and went to bed. I was a bit tipsy that evening. Then I completely forgot about it."

"There's so many hypodermic needles in here, different sizes. Some used. Some not." Carol hands the satchel back to Dennis.

"I'll hold onto it. I can check it for fingerprints and see what comes up." Dennis rubs his bald head, staring at the satchel, then places it under his seat. "Let's play trivia. We've got a little while before we get to Lynora's." Dennis opens the notes app on his phone.

"Yay!" Estelle claps her hands just like my granddaughter Lydia does when she's excited.

"What's today's category?" Filomena asks.

"Deadly insects and reptiles." Dennis reads question number one. "Which arachnid often kills after mating?"

"Easy, black widow," Filomena shouts out.

"Yes." Then Dennis adds, "Also the wolf spider and the Australian redback spider as well."

"The past few cases we've had, the women have been the perpetrators. Maybe nature is telling us something," Estelle suggests.

Bill mumbles, "Yeah, look how many men Diana has killed off over the years."

"What *is* your problem, Bill? Are you trying to be funny or hurtful? I can't tell," I say, gritting my teeth, trying my best not to get angry. What is it with this guy? He loves to pick on me.

"I'm kidding. I'm kidding." Bill glares at Estelle. "Don't hit me. I'll be good."

"You better be." Estelle shoots him a death stare. "You're jealous."

"Who? Me? No, I'm not. I'm happy for Diana," says Bill, feigning his best fake smile.

"Yes. You are. You're jealous. You need a woman, Bill. When was the last time you went on a date?"

"Um, I don't know . . . it's been a while, I guess," Bill admits.

"It's obvious you could use some female attention," says Estelle.

"Well . . . maybe I'd be in better spirits if *you* would go out with me—but you won't."

"For good reason," says Filomena. "Leave her be."

Bill squirms in his seat. "Next question, Dennis, please . . . help a brother out, would ya?"

"Sure, next question. Which state has the greatest rattlesnake population? Utah, New Mexico, Texas, California, Arizona, or Florida?"

"Tough one," I say. "I know it's not here. We find very few rattlers in our sugar fields."

"I think Utah and California get too cold for snakes to thrive," Filomena suggests.

"I'm going to guess New Mexico; it's right by the border of Mexico, and the climate seems right," says Estelle.

Carol says, "Or it could be Arizona. The Grand Canyon is there, and so much of the land is untouched by humans, so rattlers could easily thrive there."

"Right. Arizona." Dennis tells the driver to drop us off in front of the restaurant but to park across the street. "Last question. Which of the following is not an invasive species in Florida? The Burmese python, feral pigs, Cuban tree frogs, green iguanas, African snails, cane toads, armadillos, or the American alligator."

"Armadillos," Carol blurts out while collecting her things as the bus stops.

"Feral pigs," Estelle guesses.

The bus stops, and the hydraulic door opens. "We're here," Dennis announces. "The answer is the American alligator is not an invasive species. They're native and endangered. Well, used to be endangered, until 1987 anyway. Now they're just an annoyance."

We hop off the bus just in time for our 7 p.m. reservation. Everyone is dressed so nicely. It's always lovely to see Filomena and Estelle step out of their usual matching tracksuits. They're both wearing jeans and sweaters with short boots. Filomena in a red sweater and Estelle in a yellow sweater. This might be the first time they appear to be not matching at all.

Carol looks pretty in a colorful boho summer dress and sandals. Bill and Dennis are wearing pants and Tommy Bahama shirts. I'm also dressed in jeans and a sweater for the evening, since I was told we'd be sitting outside, and the weather is still a bit chilly in the evenings.

The waitress greets us with the one question we were all waiting to hear. "Can I get any of you a cocktail while you're deciding on what to order?"

Bill answers the waitress with the rhetorical question, "Does Tom Cruise do his own stunts?"

Carol answers. "Yes, of course, as far as we know, but he's getting old like the rest of us . . . so his days of jumping out of aircraft and leaping off skyscrapers are numbered."

Estelle tells the waitress, "Don't mind Bill, here. Of course we would like a cocktail. Many, actually."

"Which is your favorite specialty cocktail?" Dennis asks the waitress.

"I recommend the Italian Margaritas. It's made with Casamigos Blanco and Limoncello. It's delicious."

"Let's start with a round of Italian Margaritas then, please. What is your name?" Dennis asks.

"Mandy."

Bill begins to sing the Barry Manilow song. "Oh, Mandy, you kissed me and stopped me from shaking."

"Stop, Bill, you're scaring her," Estelle warns.

"Can't a dude have any fun anymore?"

"Nope. She's half your age." Estelle narrows her eyes at Bill.

"That's okay. He's cute," Mandy says. "He reminds me of my father, and I'm not as young as I look." She shoots a smile in Bill's direction. "I'll be right back with your drinks."

"I think she likes me." Bill smirks.

"I think her exact words were 'He reminds me of my father,' " I repeat, which makes everyone laugh.

"What's wrong with that? I can make an excellent father figure. Girls are into that these days." Bill opens up his Instagram and shows a few pictures of older guys with their young girlfriends. "See?"

"Who are these people? How do you know them? Are you stalking them? You've got too much time on your hands, Bill," Carol says with an edge in her voice.

When the drinks arrive, Dennis toasts. "To another successful case closed." We all clink and sip.

"Alright, recap the Mabel case for us." Carol taps her fingers on the table, anxiously awaiting the results.

"First, I'd like to thank Diana." Dennis nods in my direction. "Because of her, we were able to get the funding needed to send the knife to the lab for the expensive testing of the degraded DNA. The DNA came back as XX, female. We could not match it to any female in our system. We were able to match a relative to her DNA, a brother who was in the system for armed robbery. He served eight years in prison for his crime at Martin Correctional Institution. It turns out his sister was married to the milkman. My guess is that Mabel may have been having an affair with the milkman. His wife found out, stabbed her in her home, then fled the scene."

"Where is she now?"

"She is dead. The milkman is dead, and the incarcerated brother is dead. But circumstantial evidence would lead you to believe that this would be the most likely outcome of events."

"It's amazing what DNA evidence can reveal," Carol says, taking a sip of her margarita.

Estelle reveals, "You know, Filomena and I just recently got our own DNA testing done. We were adopted, so we had little information about our family history. It turns out, we are one quarter Filipino, one quarter Chinese and one half a mixed bag of everything else, including Ashkenazi Jewish. The things you can find out about your family tree these days are remarkable."

"So true." Carol perks up. "I found out I'm forty percent French. Suddenly I'm buying more French wine, and learning more about the culture."

"I can teach you the kiss." Bill wiggles his eyebrows.

"You wish." Carol's smirk turns into a smile. She's flattered by Bill's comment.

"So what happens with the case now?" Filomena asks.

"Just like all the others. We're done here." Dennis adjusts himself in his seat. "We've done our job. The boys in blue take it from here."

"Maybe the homeowner can get some peace now," Estelle suggests. "If that house is haunted, how would the ghost know the case has been resolved?"

"No idea. The homeowner can have her own little ghostly chat with her on her own time," Dennis says, looking past Estelle toward the waitress heading our way.

"I hope Mabel finds the light. Cheers to Mabel. May you rest in peace." We clink and sip as Mandy returns to take our order. I love her uniform. Her shirt reads Legalize Marinara. Very funny.

"Are you ready to order?" Mandy asks.

Bill asks her, "If we ate pasta, then antipasta in that order, would we still be hungry?"

Mandy laughs so hard that she makes him repeat the question to two other waitresses, who also enjoy the joke.

We're ordering arancino di riso and calamari fritti for appetizers and another round of drinks when Bill asks the waitress, "Since I remind you so much of your father, maybe you and I can go to bingo or trivia night one night next week?"

"I'm not into games," she says flatly.

"Well then, I'm a fantastic surfer. I'd love to bring you out to Jensen Beach sometime. The waves have been spectacular lately."

"That's more my speed." She winks at him.

"You smell like butterscotch," he tells her. She blushes and then walks away.

Estelle takes a one-dollar bill out of her bra, unfolds it, and drags it across the table to Filomena.

"What's going on here? Are you betting on me?"

"You guys are not the only ones who can make bets around here." Estelle shrugs.

"What did you bet on?" Bill scratches his head.

"None of your business," Filomena answers.

"Tell me." Bill frowns.

"Filomena bet me you would flirt with her during appetizers," Estelle explains. "I bet on something else. Let's see if I get my dollar back."

"High stakes here." Dennis fidgets in his seat. He's too big for these chairs, but he's making do the best he can.

"Tell me your bet." Bill nudges Estelle with his elbow.

"Nope," Estelle says, shaking her head.

Who needs reality TV? There's plenty of drama with this group of misfits to keep me entertained without any commercial interruptions.

"Surfing?" I ask Bill. "At your age, still?"

Carol adds, "I'm out of breath tying my shoes."

"Yoga," Bill says. "You did pretty well on that mechanical horse. I doubt you're out of breath tying your shoes."

"What?" I ask.

"Yoga. Estelle, Filomena, and I take the sunrise class every morning. Because of yoga, I'm stronger and can breathe better. That's my secret," Bill confesses. "Gotta stay strong."

"Huh!" I glare down at my swollen ankles and wonder if maybe I'll give yoga a chance. After all, 2025 is the year to try new things.

For dinner, the men share the Americano pizza, the twins order the gnocchi, and Carol and I order the fettuccini Bolognese.

Carol suggests, "Ocean's Edge is planning a disco party next Saturday night. I propose we make it a celebration of life for Tom. He loved disco. Maybe we could do a cocktail hour before the dance to honor him. What do you think?"

"Great idea," the twins say in unison.

"Alright. I'll discuss it with the office staff and see what they say," Carol decides. "I'll make the arrangements."

"I've got to do some shopping. I'm not sure what to wear. I don't have any disco attire in my wardrobe," I say. I make a mental note to call Rebecca in the morning for help.

"That's one of the best parts about retirement—all the parties and shopping for new clothes to wear to them. It's so fun," says Estelle.

For dessert, Italian cheesecake is delivered with a round of espresso martinis and a note for Bill.

"For me." Bill snatches the note quickly and reads, "It was a pleasure serving you this evening. Stay in touch. Mandy 772-555-1367."

Estelle beams with delight.

Filomena shrugs and lets out a loud, exasperated sigh. She takes the one-dollar bill, slides it back across the table to Estelle, then slams her hands against the table, rattling the martini glasses. "You win. Gosh darn it! Snickerdoodle fudge!"

Bill pulls a butterscotch candy out from his man bun and leaves it on the table for Mandy.

Chapter Thirty-Four

Theo

Every night before bed, I turn on the lighthouse my mom bought me for my eighth birthday. It's served me well over the years, keeping me safe from all that could harm me.

I've lived a long life. I'm educated and have gained a wealth of life experience through various jobs. I've solved crimes and removed evil from society. The year is 2025, and I'm feeling tired. Although I'm old, I'm too restless to embrace the sedentary lifestyle that many retirees long for.

My move to Ocean's Edge was supposed to be peaceful and uneventful. It turned out to be quite the opposite. One would think that in a fifty-five plus community, people would settle down to enjoy life at a slower pace. You'd be wrong. In these communities, or at least in this one, folks ramp things up a notch, almost as if they're making up for lost time. It's as though everything they may have missed while they were married or raising kids is what they now desire most. Booze, food, late-night parties, sex with strangers, illegal drugs—the "Do it all before you die" mantra. Not that there's anything wrong with that. Everything in moderation, as they say . . . but if you've had demons festering within for many years, be cautious. In these later years, those demons grow horns—watch out!

What do they say about idle hands and the devil's playground? I can tell you that trauma waits for stillness. Sometimes, for those who don't seek help in their early years, demons rear their ugly heads when the hustle and bustle of everyday life winds down, leaving you alone with your monster.

Dear Reader,

Feb 10th, 1998

Stanley was the first resident I met when I moved into The Ocean's Edge. We had breakfast together before I went to work. I started my new and favorite career in 1998. I'll talk more about that later.

Stanley was friendly enough. Single, like myself. Seemed a bit off, though. He spent a lot of time in the playground at Indian RiverSide Park during the after-school hours. I sat in my car one afternoon, watching him. He sat on a bench and watched the kids play. No one would give him a second once over. The elderly are often overlooked as harmless. I know otherwise.

The following afternoon, while he was at the park, I broke into his townhouse only to find a box full of naked photographs of very young boys under his bed.

In his closet, above his luggage, was a shoebox. Inside the shoebox were newspaper clippings of missing boys in Georgia and North Carolina. I took the box home with me to do some due diligence and cross-referencing to make sure this Stanley was living in and around those areas at the same time these young boys went missing.

A week later, in the middle of the night, I snuck into Stanley's townhouse and did what had to be done.

Chapter Thirty-Five

Diana
Baking with Rebecca

Rebecca spent the entire day with me. First, we baked a sugar cream pie for Tom's celebration of life. Then we settled upon an outfit to wear for this evening's disco shindig. I'd be lost without her. I thank the Lord and my negotiating skills for Rebecca each and every day.

Don't retire without a Rebecca. That's my advice. Everyone should be lucky enough to have an assistant —a helper—and she's the best. I know Rebecca's days with me are numbered since I'll be married one day soon (although no date has been set). I'm going to enjoy every moment I have left with her.

I'm going to be a retired wife with a newly retired husband. Jeb will be husband number six. Good grief! Who would have imagined in seventy-five years I'd make my way through six husbands? Since no one really knows about husband number one, let's just pretend Jeb is husband number five. For all intents and purposes, husband number one didn't really count anyway. It didn't last long enough. If there's a five-second rule for food dropping on the floor, there must surely be a one-week rule for a marriage annulment.

Since I'll be married once again, I guess I'll learn how to cook a few things this time around. To be honest, grilled cheese, tomato soup, macaroni and cheese, and Orville Redenbacher microwave popcorn are about all I've ever mastered on my own. I had a live-in chef while I was raising Lola during the demanding days at the sugar company.

I'm looking forward to learning how to fix up some good ol' Southern fried chicken and casseroles my granny used to bake.

Today we're tackling an old sugar plantation recipe, sugar cream pie, from Granny's recipe book, dated Christmas 1955. Before we start, I make tea with honey, lemon, and a pinch of Laird's apple brandy for the two of us. My granny called this a hot toddy. What is it they say in Key West? It's five o'clock somewhere. R.I.P., Jimmy Buffett.

My granny's sugar cream pie is a simple recipe, although we took a shortcut with the piecrust because it was too much work. Rebecca bought one at Publix. The pie filling requires flour, vanilla, nutmeg, salt, light cream, heavy cream, cinnamon, and three types of sugar: white, light brown, and dark brown.

While the pie is baking, Rebecca hands me a few outfits to try on. I don't have to. As soon as I see the Vince Camuto silver metallic knit jumpsuit, I know I will wear it. Easy peasy—decision rendered. She paired it with silver two-inch wedge heels. Oh, how I wish I could wear higher wedges, but my ankles have seen better days. I can't walk for long in elevated shoes anymore, let alone disco dance.

"I love that ensemble. Go try it on," Rebecca urges.

When I return, she's texting and smiling.

"What are you smiling about?" I ask.

"Oh, I'm just texting with my new boyfriend," she says, handing me disco ball dangle earrings to match my outfit.

"I love these. Thank you. They match perfectly. New boyfriend? What happened to Brian?"

"Who cares? I've moved on."

"Tell me about this one." I focus. I'm all ears.

"His name is Tamryn."

"Terrible name," I blurt out. "Sounds like a pretentious boob." I couldn't help myself. What is it with moms naming their kids weird names these days? Whatever happened to good ol' Tom, Dick, or Harry?

"It's different, sure. It's strangely fitting, though. He's unique. He's also forty-five."

"Hold on. Forty-five. Sugar bear, he's too old for you. What do you beautiful young gals see in these older men? Please tell me, because I certainly do not understand this phenomenon."

"Well, men—no . . . boys—my age are like babies. They lack direction. They don't know what they want from life, they require far too much attention, and they don't respect working women. Their mommies coddle them. They're a bunch of titty suckers!"

"Titty suckers?" I laugh; that's really funny. "So tell me about Tamryn. I want to know everything."

"Well, he never married, so I got lucky there, him being forty-five and all. He didn't marry because he took over his dad's company and didn't have much time to date. You know, just like you did."

"I'll interrupt you here, young lady. I took over my grandad's company, but I found plenty of time to play with many men, so no . . . not the same."

"Okay. Maybe not exactly the same. Anyway, he sold that company, and now he's a partner in a firm that invests in green energy technology, which includes not just solar but also air. It's complicated. I don't fully understand it, but he's interesting and treats me well. So far, so good."

"So far, so good. What does that mean?"

"It means we've had a few nice dates. He says he wants to settle down and have kids but doesn't mind if his future wife has a career, which I love to hear."

"What are your plans for the future after you finish helping me?"

"I am returning to school to study design and would like to specialize in high-end interior design, which includes hotels, condominiums, and corporate multiuse facilities."

"You will be a star." I beam with pride as if she were my own daughter. Her style and taste for design are exquisite, and she'll succeed wherever she applies herself.

The oven beeps three times, indicating that the pie is ready. Rebecca takes it out of the oven and allows it to rest on the stove.

"Don't touch this," she warns. "Allow it to cool for a few hours. I'll check in with you tomorrow. Have a great time tonight."

"Alright. Before you leave me for good, we've got shopping to do and cooking to learn, and I want you to join me in some yoga classes. I hear it's great for mobility and flexibility, and if I'm going to have a new husband soon . . . well, you know what I mean . . ."

When Rebecca leaves, I decide to take a short nap before this evening's festivities. **Naps are underappreciated;** let it be known in big, bold letters. Naps prevent burnout, lessen stress, improve memory, boost the immune system, enhance creativity, and reduce fatigue. However, you must remember to keep them short—thirty minutes will suffice. Anything longer will ruin your nighttime rest.

Chapter Thirty-Six

Diana
Disco Dance Party

The light reflects off my disco dangle earrings as I stand in front of the full-length mirror. The effect is dazzling and dynamic. The earrings send off sharp, flickering sparkles that glimmer across the room. The constant motion grabs attention and exudes retro-glam, party-ready vibes. I feel like a star—ready for the stage. Maybe in another life. But for fun, I imagine for just a moment that I'm Cher, ready to perform "If I Could Turn Back Time" one last time before I retire. I grab my hairbrush and tell Siri to play her 1999 hit song and enjoy a little dance party fantasy before heading out the door with my sugar cream pie.

"You look stunning," the twins shout in unison as I arrive through the doors at the country club.

"Thank you." My smile beams. It's been a while since I felt pretty. The twins are wearing purple sequin dresses and matching purple earrings. On any other day, the purple eyeshadow and lilac lipstick would seem overly dramatic, but today they look spectacular and perfectly fitting for the occasion.

"Where's Jeb?" asks Filomena as I place my pie on the dessert table.

"He's with his son this weekend. They are packing up his condo, getting it ready to sell. He'll be moving in with me soon."

"Are you going to have a big, fabulous wedding? I want to help plan it." Estelle claps her hands in excitement.

"Me too," Filomena chimes in.

"I believe I've attended enough weddings for a lifetime. Perhaps just a small celebration would be best."

"I disagree," Estelle challenges. "This is the celebration of marrying your soulmate. It should be an extravagant and joyous occasion. By the way, the pie looks delicious. What did you make?"

"It's a sugar cream pie. My grandma's recipe. Rebecca helped me make it," I explain.

"Rebecca? Is that redheaded sexpot here tonight?" Bill interrupts us. He and Dennis are wearing bell-bottom pants and long-sleeved striped polyester shirts with gold chains.

"No," I answer. "You two don't look like you are in costume. Are you both wearing old seventies clothes from your own wardrobe?"

Dennis admits, "Bill and I raided an old storage unit I've had for over thirty years. These are some of my old party clothes from back in the day."

"Spiffy," says Estelle.

"Far out," adds Filomena.

"You two look more like two wild and crazy guys from that *Saturday Night Live* sketch if you ask me," I say. "Truth be told, this era actually suits you both."

A giant disco ball dangles from the ceiling, delighting the senses, and the dance floor is lit up like the movie *Saturday Night Fever*. Each square illuminates at different intervals, dancing along with the music. The DJ is playing "The Hustle," and the retirees are lining up.

Estelle yanks my arm and drags me to the dance floor. "I don't remember this dance," I protest.

"Just follow along. It's not hard." She positions herself in front of me, and before I know it, a few songs later, we're still out on the dance floor, line dancing to Tina Turner's "Nutbush City Limits." She was right; line dances are pretty easy to follow. Any beginner can join in. What fun!

The DJ stops the music, and Filomena takes the stage.

"Hello, everyone, and thank you all for coming. The disco party is our most popular themed event, and this year I wanted to take a moment to celebrate Tom's life. We were all touched by Tom in one way or another, both literally or figuratively. He will be missed around here. He cared for all our residents and made himself available to help any of us whenever we were in need. In his memory, I'd like everyone to take to the dance floor for his favorite song, 'Sex Bomb' by Tom Jones."

Indeed, everyone dances to the hit song by Tom Jones in his memory.

"Let's take a spin on the dance floor in Tom's memory," suggests Bill.

Bill grabs me by the hand and waist and drags me to the dance floor while the twins follow behind with Dennis. "Be careful with those hands of yours, Bill, if you'd like to keep all of those lovely porcelain teeth of yours," I warn.

When the song concludes, Carol appears with her arms full of drinks.

"When did you get here?" asks Dennis.

"I just snuck in. It's been a busy day at the clinic." Carol is wearing a short pink metallic dress. It's nice to see Carol all gussied up. I'll bet she looks forward to getting out of those scrubs for these theme parties.

"I love your dress," I compliment her.

"I actually wore this at Studio 54." She sets the drinks on a cocktail table.

"Really?"

"Yes. Sorry I didn't meet you all out on the dance floor. This dress is too short for dancing." Carol slides the drinks off to us, one by one. "The bartender was inspired to create a cherry-flavored cocktail in Tom's honor. It's called The Tomfoolery."

"Wonder where he got the idea for that name?" I ask.

Filomena and Estelle send a wink my way.

"I loved your little speech about Tom." Carol glares at Filomena. "We were all touched by Tom, one way or another, literally or figuratively—nice touch!"

"I thought so." Filomena shrugs.

Bill rolls his eyes while Dennis looks away.

"Have you tried any of the desserts?" Carol asks.

"I made a sugar cream pie. You'll have to taste it," I suggest.

"Too late. Fat Harriett ate most of it—just kidding. I'm kidding. Don't be mad. She ate the German chocolate cake instead."

Carol looks under the cocktail table to see Mr. Anderson lying at her feet. "What is it, Mr. Anderson?" she asks the cat. "Would you like a bit of Key lime pie?" Carol saunters over to the dessert table, with Mr. Anderson following behind.

"It's uncanny how those two can understand each other," Bill points out. "She is going to be lost without Tom. They spent a lot of time together before he passed. I hope she's doing okay. She must really miss him. She's got to feel a little lonely."

Estelle offers, "I'll make a point to spend some time with her in the coming days to see how she's coping with Tom's death."

"How about you, Bill? Are you lonely these days? Did the waitress take you up on your surfing date?" I ask.

"Yes siree. She sure did. She liked surfing, but she really enjoyed riding my longboard." Bill wiggles his eyebrows and smirks devilishly.

"Really? On the first date?" I'm not sure why I bother asking.

"No. I wish. The waves were too rough to ride, there was no surfing of any kind, but we enjoyed a few cocktails out on Jensen Beach under a beautiful waxing crescent moon and a sky full of stars."

"How romantic." Filomena throws out a few kissy gestures.

Dennis walks away from the table toward the dessert table.

Carol and Dennis chat for quite some time while the rest of us dance to "A Night to Remember" by Shalamar and "Shame" by Evelyn "Champagne" King.

By the evening's end, a Donna Summer drag queen impersonator takes to the stage to lip-sync to "MacArthur Park" and the finale song "Last Dance." The whole crowd is hootin' and hollerin', and the evening's shindig has come to a close.

When we say our goodbyes, dizzy from too many Tomfooleries, feet throbbing in pain, and mentally labeling this evening as one of the most fun nights of my retirement—and perhaps my life—the evening is about to take a dark turn.

Dennis stays late to help stack the chairs and move the cocktail tables so the cleaning staff can clean the floors early the next morning. That was the last time he was seen alive.

Chapter Thirty-Seven

Diana
A Premonition

My eyes pop open in the middle of the night. The clock on my nightstand reads 4:23 a.m. A strange sense of dread washes over me. I feel cold, paralyzed, like a frigid ocean wave hitting me slowly before creeping into my chest. The air thickens, and my breathing feels shallow. Behind my eyes, I sense a weight, as if something unseen is watching me, waiting for me. My thoughts become scattered. Every sound in my bedroom suddenly feels unfamiliar, strange—either too loud or too quiet. The world probably hasn't changed, but somehow everything feels wrong.

I have difficulty falling back asleep. I stare blankly at the ceiling as the fan whirs round and round, doing its job and going about its duty without a care in the world. I notice splash marks from the champagne Jeb and I popped open a few nights ago. I miss him. He should be here. Soon he'll be right here beside me, and I'll never have to wake up alone and frightened again. That thought makes me angry because I'm a seventy-five-year-old grown ass woman and I don't need a man to protect or soothe me, but at the same time, I long for him like he's the single missing piece to my one-thousand-piece puzzle.

I decide to get up and make a hot toddy. I can't seem to shake the uneasy feeling in my chest. I fill the kettle with tap water and place it on the stove to heat up while I get dressed. I return to the kitchen just as the teakettle whistles. Perfect timing.

As I'm pouring the water into my teacup, I catch movement outside my kitchen bay window with my peripheral vision. It startles me. I overpour the water, and it spills onto the counter and floor. I quickly drop the teacup and kettle on the counter and rush to the window to find Carol and Mr. Anderson walking past my townhouse toward the park. She's talking to the cat and mumbling to herself. I see her lips moving, but my windows are closed, so I can't hear what she's saying. They're up quite early this morning after last night's disco dance fever festivities, which kept us up until nearly 2 a.m.

I quickly clean the kitchen and sit on the front porch with my hot toddy. Hopefully, the whiskey will provide me with a little morning jolt of happiness to offset the uneasiness I feel for no particular reason.

I place my right foot on an empty Adirondack chair. It's more swollen than usual, likely from all that dancing last night. I will need to hydrate and take it easy on my feet today. I'm not sure what I have going on with my old lady feet, so I asked Dr. Google. It's probably either gout or edema. I make a mental note to make a doctor appointment soon. A memory floods in and makes me smile. My father used to poke fun of my grandfather. He would say, "Every time that man stands up, it sounds like someone's trying to open a haunted treasure chest."

I observe two squirrels racing around the trunk of an oak tree. In the dim blue hues of morning, flashes of fur loop higher within the tree with each pass. They squawk at each other, then race around the tree again like little children playing the childhood game of tag.

As the morning progresses and the sun begins to rise, my uneasiness descends from my chest to the pit of my stomach. Something terrible approaches. I can sense it. This feeling is familiar to me—the moment in the boardroom when something shifts and control is either lost or seized. It's a flicker in time. You feel the balance tilt. All eyes are on you. A moment that alters the trajectory of the future.

Then, a group text from Carol.

911

Come to the country club NOW
Dennis is dead

Chapter Thirty-Eight

Diana
Murder at The Ocean's Edge

I race over as fast as my swollen feet can take me, and still I'm the last to arrive. Dennis is already covered, on the gurney, and on the way out of the country club when a lady detective approaches the four of us.

"Hello, I'm Detective Anita Crow." She introduces herself and offers her hand to shake all of ours. She has two black braids. She's very tall, Native American, with a stern face. She appears very no-nonsense. We all shake her hand and introduce ourselves, but no one utters another word. Estelle is crying softly into a handkerchief, and Bill is consoling her and rubbing her back.

"Can we sit down for a moment?" Detective Crow asks while directing another officer to keep the other residents away.

"Sure." Carol answers for all of us as we sit.

"I'll not waste your time here. I know who you all are. I know you were close. I know about the cold case crimes. I know Dennis may have enemies. What

I need from all of you is the timeline. Can we walk through it?" Detective Crow takes out a notepad and pen from her jacket pocket.

Carol begins. "Last night, we had a disco dance party, which was also a celebration of life for a fellow resident, Tom, who recently passed away."

"What time did the event end?" the detective asks.

Bill scratches his bun and says, "Well, the DJ stopped playing music around midnight, but people lingered until one a.m. The five of us stayed to clean up until maybe one-thirty or so."

"Is that so?" The detective glares into each of our eyes, one by one, until we answer yes.

"I walked home alone around one-thirty," I say.

Filomena says, "Estelle and I walked home together shortly after Diana left."

Bill adds, "I helped Dennis fold chairs and move a few tables so that the cleaners could clean the floors in the morning. Then I left."

"What about you, Carol?" asks the detective.

"Mr. Anderson—um, the cat—and I left after Bill," Carol says, looking at the detective straight in the eye like she was being challenged to a staring contest.

"So you were the last to see Dennis alive?"

"If you say so . . . I guess." Carol fidgets in her chair.

"How exactly did he die?" I ask, and I'm sure everyone in the room is wondering the same thing. I can see the blood on the floor. The disco ball, now lowered to the dance floor, has a bloody knife stuck in the side of it, but no one has declared the cause of death.

With a stone-cold face, the detective says, "I'll not divulge that information at this time, as we investigate. Can someone direct me to the person who can get me the keys to his townhouse?"

"Sure." Carol gets up from the table to retrieve the key from the office.

"Let's go!" The detective gestures for us to follow her.

"All of us?" I ask.

"Yes. All of you." It isn't an ask, but rather a demand. I'm sure we couldn't say no. "We're all going to his townhouse. I may have questions about what I find, and you may be able to help me."

Just as we follow Detective Crow to Dennis's townhouse, a news alert from the Nextdoor app hits my phone. Good news travels fast, but in a small Southern town, bad news travels faster than a hot knife through butter. The news alert reads "Murder at The Ocean's Edge."

Chapter Thirty-Nine

Diana
The Journal

On the walk to Dennis's townhouse, Bill grumbles quietly to me. "She thinks we're suspects. This is malarkey! She doesn't need our help! She wants to analyze us. Don't piss on my leg and tell me it's raining, woman."

"Yeah, I don't trust her either," I admit. "I bet she just wants to get our reaction to what she may uncover inside. Also . . . what does the other detective do? He follows her around like a hungry puppy dog."

Detective Crow walks rapidly with long determined steps while her sidekick follows behind. When we arrive at Dennis's townhouse, the young male, barely a twenty-year-old lackey, fumbles with the key until Detective Crow snatches it from his hand and opens the door herself.

I remark under my breath, for only my friends to hear, "He's as useful as a chocolate teakettle." We laugh. We need a bit of levity at the moment, so no apologies for the bad joke.

The townhouse exudes the scent of lemons and fresh linen. It's immaculate. The sink is empty, and the dishes are neatly put away. His home appears unoccupied, as if it's ready to be featured in *Southern Living* magazine, were there ever an issue for a fifty-five plus community townhouse.

He has a vast collection of lighthouses, specifically Florida lighthouses. I wasn't aware that he was a collector. There are many of them, all lined up in the living room bookcase, still illuminated. I guess they're still on since he never returned home last night to turn them off. You can tell that these lighthouses are his pride and joy because not a speck of dust can be found on any of them.

Filomena and Estelle walk over to each lighthouse and inspect them. Filomena turns them off one by one. "They're lovely."

"Such detail." Estelle reads some of the plaques below the lighthouses. "Alligator Reef Lighthouse, Florida Keys; Gasparilla Lighthouse, Gasparilla Island; St. Augustine Lighthouse, St. Augustine."

Carol turns to Bill and says, "You're going to be lost without him."

"How lost?" Bill eggs her on.

"As lost as last year's Easter egg," Carol jokes. Then she adds, "Without him, you won't be able to find your ass even with both hands in your back pocket."

Detective Crow glares at Carol and Bill with furious eyes. "That's so inappropriate. What's wrong with you people? Your friend died and you're making jokes."

"Too soon?" Carol shrugs.

"No, Dennis would have loved that," Bill explains to the detective. "It's sarcasm and dark humor between us friends. Like you, we're exposed to death every day; we work on cold cases, and sometimes humor helps ease the pain. When it comes to a friend, it's even more painful, so a bit of levity can help us get through this terrible task. We're all in shock. We will grieve later."

"I found something," the young male detective shouts from the bedroom.

He's holding a journal when we arrive. "I found it on the nightstand." He explains that the journal he is holding was positioned next to another lighthouse. This lighthouse is older than the others and has a vintage quality. The plaque below reads "Cape Florida Lighthouse, Key Biscayne."

"Are you sure we should be reading his personal journal?" I ask.

Bill snatches the journal from the young detective's hand. "I'm his best friend. I'll read it." He reaches into the front pocket of his shorts to pull out his reading glasses, places them on his face, rifles through the pages, and settles upon the last page. "I'll read his last entry first."

"Go ahead," urges Detective Crow.

"May third, 2025. Twenty-two lighthouses—twenty-two people eradicated from the Earth—my life's purpose. I'm proud of the work I accomplished, although a few, unfortunately and regrettably, got caught up in the crosshairs. I'll have to suffer for that one day, but no life is lived without flaws."

"What does that mean? Lighthouses? People? I'm confused," I say. "Go back."

"Hold on. There are dates in the journal. Let me skim through. Let's see if I can find dates from his time here at Ocean's Edge." Bill sits on the corner of Dennis's bed, taking his time to find entries to read while we stand frozen in silence, like statues, awaiting an explanation for the final passage in his journal and a reason someone may want Dennis dead.

"Let's move over to the dining room table, shall we? No need to stand around while Bill reads," Detective Crow suggests. Her eyebrows furrow. She looks annoyed, and all color has been leached from her face. She's putting on her game face.

"Good idea," I say, but I know full well from my boardroom days that she likely suggested this because an oval dining room table makes it easier to read everyone's faces simultaneously.

Filomena rummages through the kitchen cabinets for water glasses and hands everyone a glass of filtered water from the refrigerator as we sit at the dining room table.

I take a quick look around the dining room before sitting down. Dennis has beautiful plants strategically placed throughout his home to create a warm atmosphere. Upon closer inspection, I notice they're fake. They appear alive until you get close enough to realize that they lack a scent. They offer a warm, cozy feeling on the outside, yet are scentless and dead on the inside. Internally I wonder if the plants might be a metaphor for Dennis's life.

As we settle down and Bill begins to speak, everyone seems a little nervous and fidgety in their seats. Carol appears especially edgy. She scratches her wrist, then her neck, and blinks hard as if something is bothering one of her eyes. She rubs her right eye and lets out a big sigh.

Bill opens the journal and reads another entry.

"February second, 1998. This is the day I joined the Martin County Sheriff's Office Special Operations Division. I was a perfect fit for Special Investigations (VICE) due to my background in investigative journalism. In twenty-five years on the force, there wasn't a crime my team couldn't solve. On the rare occasion we manipulated evidence to get our man, the ends always justified the means, and I have no regrets.

"I moved into The Ocean's Edge with the money I stole from a corrupt FBI agent during my days as a journalist. My final career choice as a special agent detective was my most rewarding. There is nothing quite like having complete control over taking down society's filth with my own team by my side. When my team and I couldn't take them down through legal means, I resorted to my old faithful—needles full of heroin, fentanyl, or propofol, depending on the circumstances.

"I learned all about needles from my junkie mom. It became my MO only after ending the life of my father with a cake knife was too bloody for my liking."

Bill stops reading here. He looks up at all of us. We're stunned. I'm stunned. I don't have any real emotion right now. I can't feel anything. I feel like I'm in a dream. How is any of this real? I'm a pretty good judge of character. Dennis is a killer? It can't be. How can this be? How was he able to so carefully weave us into this web of deceit?

Bill skims through several pages on his own, reading quietly to himself.

Estelle asks, "Why would Dennis write such things? If true, it's incriminating."

"Don't sociopaths like to get credit for their work? Like a form of approval?" I share only what I've gathered from watching crime shows on TV.

"I'm going to need to take that journal down to the station," Detective Crow says. She reaches for the journal, but Bill pulls it away from her.

"Not yet. Dennis has entries about residents at Ocean's Edge: Stanley, a pedophile whom he killed; Beverly; Henry, the chess player; Paul, the gardener."

Detective Crow stands up from the table, snatches the journal from Bill's hand, and commands, "We will take this from here."

"But—" Bill's complaints fall on deaf ears. "There is more to this story."

"Surely. But perhaps not more for *you* to know," Detective Crow scolds.

"He was my best friend. I deserve an explanation." Bill's not giving up.

"I'm not sure you do." The detective folds her arms in anger.

"Yes, we all do," Filomena adds.

Detective Crow surmises, "Okay, from what I can tell, there are twenty-two lighthouses." She points to the lighthouses on the bookshelves. "Without reading the journal further, I can presume there are twenty-two deaths recorded in this journal. Also, Dennis is dead, so someone knew about what he was doing, maybe one of you. You're all suspects. Maybe one of you killed Dennis."

Estelle says with a shaky voice, holding back tears, "None of us would do such a thing. He was our friend."

Detective Crow glares at each of us and says, "I've seen many a friend kill another. In fact, it's usually a friend or family member who does you in, in the end."

"Not this time," Bill argues.

"It's time to go. We will be in touch. Or maybe we won't. Time will tell. Dennis had a stellar reputation on the Treasure Coast. I'm not sure how we're going to pursue this moving forward, to be honest."

"So what now?" Filomena asks.

"Don't call me. I'll call you." Detective Crow smirks.

"Wowza. Just like that?" Filomena shakes her head.

"So that's it?" I ask.

"That's it—for now." Detective Crow and her sidekick rush through the door, journal in hand, without looking back. We never saw either one of them ever again.

Chapter Forty

Mr. Anderson

I miss Monty every day. Pink Floyd's song "Wish You Were Here" plays in my head as rain pelts against the windows in the country club. I sit by the window and reflect on the past sixteen years here at The Ocean's Edge. Like the song, Carol and I are now two lost souls swimming in a fishbowl, year after year.

I knew all along that the deaths of Monty, Ziggy, and Tom were related. They had the same needle prick behind their ear when I found them. Sadly, because they were old and ill, autopsies were never completed. My understanding is that Ziggy was a pedophile, Monty may have been embezzling money from the community funds, and Tom was a liability that got caught up in Dennis's crosshairs. I can't forgive him for taking away my Monty. I also believe that Monty may have been onto him as well.

I was there when Dennis died. I witnessed his death. Dennis walked directly into the knife after Carol confronted him. At first, Dennis dared Carol to stab him, but she wouldn't do that. She couldn't do that. It's not her nature. She's a nurse. She could do no harm. She's too kind. Tom told her that Dennis had been up to no good and suspected he had something to do with the killings at The Ocean's Edge. Carol wanted answers, but Dennis refused to give them.

In the end, I believe I know why Dennis walked directly into the knife. I think he simply gave up. I believe he wanted to die. He wished for it all to be over. Living with what he had done . . . all the murders . . . for all those years. It weighs heavily upon the soul. The gig was up, and he knew it.

Frightened, Carol let go of the knife as Dennis fell to the floor. He was dead within moments. She yanked the knife out of his chest and wiped the handle clean with her dress. Shaking, crying, she was screaming out, "Why, Dennis? Why? It didn't have to end this way." She stuck the knife into the disco ball and mumbled, "I freaking hate disco," before yanking on the rope pulley, returning the ball back to its ceiling position.

It was Carol who called 911.

The station dispatched Detective Crow and the young detective.

A month later, when the police had yet to respond, I overheard the retirees chatting over coffee.

Diana said, "Bill and I went to the precinct for a visit."

"We needed answers," Bill clarified.

"And?" Filomena and Estelle chimed in.

"Well . . . hold onto your britches, ladies . . . there is no detective named Crow."

"What? Balderdash!" Estelle blurted out.

"We've been bamboozled," Diana admitted.

"Yes. Sadly. When we described her to the chief of police, he alluded that a woman who matched her description worked for him in the special crimes unit. She and her son recently retired and moved to a protected sanctuary on Native American land in Canada." Bill pulled a photo from his shirt pocket. It was a photo of six officers in the special crimes unit.

Filomena pointed to Detective Crow. "That's her."

"Yes. Her real name is Sandra Crawley." Bill placed the photo back into his shirt pocket.

"Did they turn in a journal they found that belonged to Dennis?" Estelle asked.

"Nope," Diana answered. "What he said was, 'I'm not sure what you're getting at here, but we have Detective Dennis Duncan's death on record as due to natural causes. Says in the case file, sudden cardiac arrest.' "

"Can't be." Estelle looked bewildered.

"Then the chief disappeared for a few minutes. He returned with the file. The official death certificate was indeed processed as sudden cardiac arrest due to sudden respiratory arrest, with the manner of death listed as natural causes. There was no autopsy. He was cremated the following day," Diana explained.

The somber look of this group has had a lasting effect on me. I'm not sure they will be the same after learning about Dennis, his killings, and the police cover-up. I wonder whether they will continue with Treasure Coast cold cases—only time will tell.

In the weeks that follow, Carol wakes up vomiting.

"It won't be long before my stage two stomach cancer gets worse," Carol tells me. "I've got to get to the oncologist soon so that I can consider all of my care options." She pats my head. She seems at peace with her diagnosis. She doesn't seem scared. "Mr. Anderson, you'll keep my secret, won't you?"

"I will keep your secret. You're my friend. I'll never tell. I will keep *all* of your secrets," I meow back.

Sadness creeps into the fine lines upon her face. I can almost feel the regret as if it's my own personal pain. Regret won't save Dennis's life or hers. Dennis did this to her. His choices led us here, not hers.

I rush to the lobby and bring her the March edition of *Scientific American* magazine. I drop it in front of her, and she browses through it curiously. She discovers an article about a promising new drug for stomach cancer. Upon finding it, I wag my tail and let out a loud "Meow." We are strong. We can fight this. We will get through this together. After all, like Bette Davis once said . . . old age is no place for sissies.

"Thank you, Mr. Anderson. You are a true friend. I will ask my doctor about it." She pats my head and smiles at me. She knows how much I love music, so she opens the Spotify app on her phone and plays Marc Cohn's "True Companion" just for me. I'm thankful to have Carol in my life. She is my best friend and a faithful companion for however long we have left together in our elder years.

Epilogue

Diana
Three Months Later

The stillness of the sunrise feels like the world is holding its breath as it makes its grand entrance to another spectacular day in South Florida.

Soft light stretches across the horizon, brushing the sky with delicate hues of gold and pink. Everything feels suspended in that moment: the trees unmoving, the air cool and hushed, as if nature itself is slowly awakening to a new day, not wanting to disturb the peace. It brings serenity, a deep sense of calm, a quiet kind of awe, and a fleeting reassurance that for at least this moment, everything is precisely as it should be.

Jeb and I wake early every morning to watch the sun's arrival from my veranda overlooking the ocean. It's one of the greatest shows on Earth, and each day is different from the last.

"Grandma!" I hear my name called from inside the house.

"Yes, sugar," I yell back. "Grandpa Jeb and I are out here enjoying the sunrise. Come on out."

Lydia emerges with her pink bunny sleeping friend, whom she calls Honey, cuddled tightly in her arms.

"Does God paint the sky every day?" she asks.

"Every day. Every day," I explain, "a different design and different colors."

"One day, I'd like to be an artist and paint a sunrise just like this one." She beams.

I grab her, give her a big bear hug, and say, "You will be an amazing artist. I am going to enjoy everything you paint. I'll be your biggest fan."

"Oh, Grandma. Not yet. I'm just a kid. I've still got kid stuff to do. But, one day, I'm going to paint with every color I can find, a great, big, gigantic sunset." Lydia stretches both arms out, gesturing to show how big.

"I'm off to the kitchen, my love, to make us some French toast," promises Jeb. He kisses Lydia on the forehead and ventures off to cook.

Lydia climbs into my lap, and my heart melts with happiness—happiness I never thought I deserved until now.

"I love you, Grandma."

"I love you too, Lydia. Thank you for visiting us this weekend. It's been the highlight of my whole year. You are my favorite person in the whole world. I just wanted you to know that."

As I reflect on the totality of my life, I remind myself that if you live long enough, you'll witness bad times alongside good times. You'll experience everything—love and joy, but also corruption, greed, and poor life choices. My poor decisions led to unfortunate choices in men. Don't let these choices make you cynical. I gave my company fifty-six years of my life, wasted my heart on unworthy men who didn't deserve my love, and never made room for lasting friendships. My family and Jeb are the silver lining in it all. Family, friendship, love—this is what matters in a life worth living. Find your passion. Find your people.

My grandfather was correct when he said that sugar is thicker than blood. However, only family and friendships bring lasting, true joy—and that's all that matters.

A few hours later, after Lola picks up Lydia, Jeb and I mosey over to the country club. Filomena, Estelle, Bill, and Carol are waiting for us.

"What are we drinking today?" I ask excitedly.

Carol already has the mugs ready on the table for our arrival, saying, "Mexican coffee today."

"What's in it?" asks Jeb.

"Tequila, coffee liqueur, a splash of coffee, whipped cream, and a pinch of cinnamon." Carol hands each of us a spoon. "I may have gone a bit overboard with the whipped cream."

"Sounds delicious." I take a quick sip and instantly feel warm and cozy inside.

"How was your visit with Lydia?" asks Bill.

"Lovely," I admit. "I already miss her."

"Grandkids are the best." Bill waves a hand around his man bun, shouts "Abracadabra!" and pulls out a quarter. "Next time she visits, I'll have to show her some of my magic tricks."

"Impressive," Jeb compliments Bill.

"Sorry about the mugs today," Carol apologizes. "I found these at a thrift store during an animal rescue event last weekend. Each mug represents a different cat breed."

Bill sighs and clears his throat. "This is a testament to how far we've fallen—from a badass group of crime fighters to a bunch of old pussies."

Mr. Anderson doesn't seem to care for that remark. He sets off a series of loud meows from beneath the table.

Estelle punches Bill in the arm. "Bad Bill."

"Ouch! You're always hitting me."

"You deserve it!" Filomena fist-bumps her sister in approval.

Bill warns Estelle with a smirk, "Keep it up and I'll cancel your birth certificate."

Estelle snaps back, "Kill me, Bill, really? You love me."

Bill blushes and shrugs. "Maybe."

Estelle reaches into her pocket and hands a note to Carol. "Before I forget, this is for you. Dennis came to me last night with a message for you. I didn't understand it, but I hope you will."

Carol opens the note and reads it out loud. "You did what had to be done, and I forgive you." Carol sobs quietly while Mr. Anderson jumps onto Carol's lap for support. We watch, but no one dares to ask any questions. This is Carol's moment to grieve, for only she knows what the message meant. Maybe one day soon she'll explain to us its meaning.

"Ahem." A short, stout gentleman approaches our table, clears his throat loudly, and says, "Hello."

Filomena says, "Oh, everyone, this is Tim. He's the new Tom."

"Hello, Tim," we all chime in one after the other.

"Hello. I have a few new retirees I'd like you to meet."

"Oh, pray tell. New playmates!" Estelle claps her hands in excitement, so enthusiastically, like she just won the big showcase on *The Price is Right*.

"Well, we have a new couple. Millie and Randall are moving in today. They're longtime Jensen Beach residents. They seem like they'll be loads of fun. I'm sure you'll give them a warm welcome."

I peek past Tim to find a beautiful older woman dressed to the nines in a pair of high-heeled wedges I could never imagine being able to walk in. She's with a thin fellow wearing a Grateful Dead T-shirt, and he's got a long gray ponytail. Another one with long hair? Who knew this was a thing with old men these days? Now I wonder if he, too, fought in a war and how many people he may have killed along the way. A giant ring of keys hangs from his jeans belt. Hmm. Interesting couple.

"And . . ." Tim continues. "Other news . . . the chief of police would like to have a word with all of you later this afternoon . . . something about a cold case?"

The End

The Retirees
Boozy Coffee Creations

Baileys Irish Coffee

2 oz Baileys Original Irish Cream
1 oz Jameson Irish Whiskey
6 oz hot coffee
A dollop of whipped cream

Velvet Bliss

2 oz Baileys Original Irish Cream
1 oz Godiva Chocolate Liqueur
1 oz vanilla vodka
6 oz hot coffee
A dash of vanilla creamer
A dollop of whipped cream

Italian Coffee

1½ oz Frangelico
6 oz hot coffee
A dash of Italian Sweet Crème by Coffee mate
A dollop of whipped cream

Amaretto Coffee

1½ oz of Amaretto liqueur
6 oz hot coffee
A dollop of whipped cream

RumChata Coffee

1½ oz of RumChata
6 oz hot coffee
A dollop of whipped cream

Pairs nicely with Nabisco's Nilla Wafers.

Mudslide

1 oz vodka
½ oz Kahlúa
½ oz Baileys
1 tsp chocolate syrup
A scoop of ice cream
Splash of coffee, optional
Ice

Blend in blender.

Italian Margarita (Lynora's Italian Restaurant)

2 oz Casamigos Blanco Tequila
½ oz Pallini Limoncello
Splash of South Beach Agave
Lemon juice
Lime juice
Ice

Shake and serve in Margarita cocktail glass with salted rim.

Hot Toddy

1½ oz Laird's Apple Brandy
Tea bag
6 oz of hot water
Honey
Lemon

Mexican Coffee

1½ oz tequila
1 oz coffee liqueur
6 oz hot coffee
A dollop of whipped cream
Cinnamon

Sugar Cream Pie (Sugar Plantation Recipe)

Store-bought pie crust
¾ cup all-purpose flour
½ cup sugar
½ cup light brown sugar
½ cup dark brown sugar
½ tsp cinnamon
¼ tsp nutmeg
¼ tsp salt
1½ cups heavy cream
1½ cups half-and-half
2 tsp vanilla extract

Preheat oven to 375 degrees Fahrenheit. Mix ingredients together in a large bowl. Pour into the pie shell. Bake for 35 to 45 minutes, or until crust is golden brown and center of the pie is set. Dust with cinnamon. Cool for 20 minutes before slicing.

Enjoy a short horror story

"Without justice, there can be no peace." -Martin Luther King, Jr.

MURDER ON MAPLE
JANET O'NEILL, LEAH ORR,
& The Ocean Breeze Book Club

Halloween 2024

A blood-orange sunrise stretches across the South Florida horizon, casting a fiery glow over the coastal skyline. Burnt orange and soft pink blend seamlessly with streaks of crimson red and gold. Wisps of clouds catch the morning light, glowing like embers against the retreating darkness of night. The fading darkness foreshadows the day ahead.

Janet had rolled out of bed this morning earlier than usual. With coffee in hand, she steps onto her balcony, savoring the stillness when the world feels freshly born. Though she has captured many sunrises over the years, few compare to witnessing Mother Nature's masterful work of art in person.

My New Jersey friends would envy this beautiful fall morning, she thinks, appreciating the warmth and color of her new life. She's thankful she made the transition from snowbird to full-time resident. Becoming a Floridian was the right call.

At 8 a.m., neighbors are already stirring. Donna is walking her two dogs, Bear and Maui, and Anne is on her way to the gym—a typical day in the neighborhood, like any other.

As Janet walks toward her car, Anne shouts out, "Remember, tonight we're celebrating Carol's sixty-fifth birthday with all the ladies from book club."

"Can't wait," Janet responds. "See you later."

Tonight's celebration will be a lot of fun. Carol is excited about her milestone birthday and her long-awaited Medicare perks.

Janet parks her car in the nearly empty parking lot and strides toward the entrance of the supermarket. Before entering, she tugs a shopping cart free from the corral. Something rolls inside the basket. At first glance, it looks like a small flesh-colored toy. Curious, she grabs her eyeglasses hanging from her Rolling Stones T-shirt and leans over the cart to inspect the strange object.

It isn't a toy. A severed woman's index finger, freshly manicured with red nail polish, sits eerily upright in the cart.

Janet freezes, standing there stunned. She opens her mouth to scream, but no sound emerges. Don't panic, she tells herself. Do something. But what?

Suddenly she hears tires screeching from the parking lot. She whips her head around to find an old, dilapidated 1970s Volkswagen camper peeling away. She takes a mental snapshot of the license plate: D3D HE4D. That won't be hard to remember.

Her heart pounds loudly in her chest as she recognizes the driver. That's Norman. She recalls playing pool with him recently at Stuart Billiards. He said something peculiar to her at the time. He admired her nails. "I love red nail polish on a woman. It's very sexy." It hadn't seemed important at the time—until now.

She quickly alerts the store manager, who contacts the police.

When the police arrive, they find blood droplets in the parking spot where the camper had been. Later, video surveillance reveals a woman struggling . . . taken from the parking lot . . . violently thrown into the van against her will.

The finger left behind feels disturbing. The finger in the cart—deliberate. A twisted clue? Perhaps a game?

Nerves frazzled and still shaken, Janet begs her friends—Donna, Anne, and Karen—to meet for drinks at Chris' Martini Bar.

"Mike," she pleads to the manager, "I'm going to need something to calm my nerves, something strong. It's been quite a day."

"What happened?" Mike reaches for a martini glass, eyebrows raised, and a look of concern on his face.

Before Janet can answer, Donna jumps in. "You're never going to believe this."

"Murder in our small town," Anne adds dramatically, stirring the day's drama.

"Well, not technically," Karen clarifies, "but . . . Janet found a bloody finger in a shopping cart, and we think it's tied to that VW camper that Norman drives around town. You know the one . . . the license plate reads D3D HE4D."

Mike shakes his head, looking dumbfounded, while continuing to mix our cocktails. "That's wild. Funny thing . . . yesterday, an old woman sat outside on the patio wearing a Grateful Dead T-shirt. She had a dog with her. I swear there was dried blood in her hair— black hair with a grey streak, if I recall correctly. She said she was staying on Maple Street."

Mike adds the ingredients into four shakers: vanilla vodka, grenadine, dry vermouth, orange bitters, and ice. He gives them a good shake and then pours the concoction into martini glasses for the ladies to enjoy.

Janet takes the first sip of the martini. "This is new. I like it. What do you call it?"

"Murder on Maple." Mike smiles, beaming with delight.

After a few rounds of drinks, Janet suggests, "Let's walk over to Maple Street and snoop around."

Outside, Kagdis, the bar's resident blonde-furred cat, lies on a patio chair. "Meow," he cries, like it's a warning.

"Be careful," Mike cautions before the women cross over Jensen Beach Boulevard toward Maple Street.

"We'll be fine," Janet replies. "It's still early, and the trick-or-treaters will be on the streets soon."

With a bit of liquid courage, the women approach Maple Street.

Janet stops cold, grabbing Anne's hand.

"There it is," mutters Janet, gripping Anne's hand tighter for support. "There it is," she repeats. "The VW van."

"What should we do?" Karen asks, grabbing Anne's other hand.

Donna suggests, "Let's go back to the martini bar."

"It's too late to turn back now," Janet adds grimly.

The four ladies stare at the van parked directly across from the restaurant at 11 Maple Street. They creep from behind as adrenaline spikes through their veins. They clutch their phones in their hands, just in case they need to call for help. As they inch closer, it becomes apparent that the van has been abandoned.

With doors ajar and windows open, a bottle of red nail polish sits upon the dashboard.

Too afraid to enter, Janet dials 911. The ladies walk toward the curb and around the corner to meet the police.

Within minutes, two police officers arrive. One is tall with a mustache, and the other is an older officer who is portly and balding. The ladies lead them toward the van, but it has vanished. Strangely, the officers don't seem surprised.

"I swear, officers," Janet insists, "the van was right there in front of 11 Maple."

"We believe you," the officer with the mustache says. "This isn't the first time."

"What do you mean?" Anne asks.

"It was here last year as well," the shorter, balding officer states. "And the year before that."

"What?" asks Karen. "What is going on around here?"

Officer Mustache explains, "A few years ago on Halloween, a fisherman spotted a pelican with a bloody sock in its beak. We also found a severed foot under the pier. A VW camper was seen fleeing the scene—later found on Maple Street. It vanished before backup arrived."

"The short, balding officer adds, "Last year, similar story. We found bloodstained underwear near the train tracks—same camper."

"Let me guess," Janet says. "It vanished before the police arrived?"

"Exactly," both officers say in unison.

The day after Halloween, candy wrappers litter the street along Maple. The old VW van is gone, and the air is calm. Janet, groggy from yesterday's mayhem followed by a long night out celebrating Carol's sixty-fifth birthday, is stopped dead in her tracks. Lying in the sunlight on the sidewalk like a warning is a bloody yellow scarf.

One week later, Janet walks along the Jensen Beach Causeway Bridge. She frequently sees an older man drawing beneath the bridge, but never peeks over to see what he's painting. The artist is well known in Jensen Beach. He's an artistic historian of sorts, painting the beauty and soul of Jensen Beach for decades. He's seen it all, this man. He's got a plethora of stories to tell. Many morning walkers stop for nostalgia, to chat with him about days gone by. Today, as she approaches him, something compels her to stop and observe his art.

The artist is sketching a VW camper van by the beach. A pool cue—its tip dusted in blue ink—protrudes from the window.

Janet is stunned by what she sees. "What is this? Do you know who owns the van?"

The artist smiles. "Sure. Norman."

"Norman?" Janet's skin begins to feel itchy. Goosebumps appear on her arms.

"Yes. He's the dishwasher at the restaurant, 11 Maple Street. He comes here often to fish. On Halloween, he must've caught something big—never saw so much blood on his shirt before."

The following day, Janet's book club gathers in the card room for an emergency meeting.

"Maybe you ladies can help crack the case of the murder on Maple." Janet recounts the facts about the finger found in the shopping cart, running into Norman at Stuart Billiards and his fascination with red nail polish, the VW camper van that disappeared, a bloody yellow scarf on the sidewalk on Maple Street, and the mysterious artist on the pier. "The police reported that the fingerprints on the severed finger did not lead to an identification, and they have no solid leads to pursue."

"What can we do?" asks Anne.

"Help me walk through the evidence," Janet continues. "This morning, on my doorstep, I found a Grateful Dead T-shirt neatly folded and a Polaroid photo of us standing on Maple Street." She places the Polaroid on the table for the ladies to investigate. Written in blue chalk under the photo are the words "You're closer than anyone has ever been."

"I think the killer is watching us," Karen says. "I think maybe Norman has been following us for weeks."

Donna adds, "He's playing with us. He wants us to be scared."

"But why me? Why us?" Janet asks.

Anne clears her throat. "Because you're finally asking the right questions."

The room falls silent. What is that supposed to mean, Janet thinks.

Donna stares at the ladies around the table, slowly, calmly, and controlled. Her eyes lock on Janet's. "Anne, show the ladies what you found."

Anne retrieves a folded newspaper clipping from her purse and places the article on the table. The headline reads "Missing: A Teenage Girl Disappears from Boarding House on Maple Street."

No one utters a word while Anne continues. "I looked up the address 11 Maple Street with county records. A woman named Evelyn Dumas ran a boarding house in the lot next to 11 Maple in the late 1970s before it became a restaurant. There were stories. Disappearances. She was never charged with a crime, but locals whispered about nefarious goings-on in that home."

"Like what, exactly?" Janet asks.

"Well," Anne elaborates, "a tenant named Rachel went missing, then another young runaway named Sandra, then Clara. There were more. Some disappeared, others were found floating in the intracoastal, or left for dead under the bridge. Clara was Norman's sister. Rumor has it Evelyn Dumas paid people to stay quiet, so no real investigation from the police ever took place."

"That's terrible," says Donna.

Anne scowls, angered by the situation. Droplets of sweat bead along her brow. "The police knew about the disappearances. Evelyn drove a VW van. The boarding house and the van were never searched or investigated." Anne takes in a deep breath, lets it go, then says, "I've got something I need to confess."

A flurry of responses ensue from the ladies: "Oh?" "What?" and "Tell us."

"I've been helping Norman," Anne admits.

"You what?" Donna demands an explanation. "Please explain."

"Why would you do that?" asks Karen. "That's asinine."

"Well . . . every Halloween for the past few years, we've been leaving clues. It was I who dropped the finger in the cart, Janet."

"What?" Janet's mouth falls open in astonishment.

"Yes. And I gave Mike at Chris' Martini Bar the idea for the cocktail, Murder on Maple. I wanted you all to follow the trail of clues. To see it. To feel it. Norman and I want to carry the story forward to someone who is not emotionally attached."

Janet says, "Anne, this is insane. Why not go to the police? Why are you helping him?"

Karen asks in a shaky voice, "Please tell me you aren't killing people, abducting women?"

"No. Every Halloween, however, we re-create the story, leaving behind a clue, a finger, a foot, a sock, a bottle of red nail polish; the same clues left behind from the 1970s crime scenes. We want the town to feel the weight of the atrocities it ignored for so long."

Donna asks, "Are you helping him kill?"

Anne smiles, cold, detached. "No, I help the town remember. The killings . . . those were Evelyn Dumas.

Norman and I have been trying to bring new attention to these cold case abductions and disappearances."

"But . . . the body parts? Where are they coming from? Why are you helping? What's in this for you?" Janet asks.

Anne replies, "Norman is my brother, and Clara was . . . well . . . she was our sister. I want justice. We're not killing anyone. The body parts are from the morgue. Norman has a friend who works there."

"Your brother? Clara is your sister? You should have told us! We could have helped you all along." Janet rubs Anne's back, comforting her.

Anne answers looking down at the floor, diverting her eyes from her friends. "I was too afraid to ask for help initially. I was not sure how well you would respond."

"So what now?" Janet asks.

Anne glances at her phone, which buzzes on the table. She answers, "He's ready. He wants to meet everyone." Anne turns toward the window, where the old, familiar VW camper van sits idling across the street.

Karen pleads, "Explain the van."

Anne clarifies, "The van once belonged to Evelyn, but Norman stole it a few years ago. We believed it was the only thing that connected the murders to

Evelyn. The police wouldn't help, so we stepped up to find our own clues. Sadly, there is no evidence of any crime in the van."

Norman enters the card room, bringing the final clue: a list of names of all the women who went missing under Evelyn Dumas's watch. There are eleven of them. "Take this to the police—demand that they investigate. Evelyn is still out there somewhere, walking freely among us. She needs to be caught."

Norman hands the group a Polaroid photo of Evelyn, revealing an old woman with black hair and a gray streak. It suddenly hits Janet that this woman was recently spotted with her dog at Chris' Martini Bar.

"Mike from the martini bar told us about a woman who looks like this photo. We've got to get this photo to the police," Janet suggests.

"The police will be of no help to you," Norman says. "They are clearly uninterested in investigating Evelyn. Just be careful. She's still out there. We're done here. It's time for us to retire . . . move on. We're getting too old for this. It's up to all of you now to catch the killer."

Before Norman and Anne depart in the VW van, Anne says, "Continue the mission. Find her, catch her, and don't let this town forget. Find justice for Clara.

You ladies are smart, brave, and resilient. You can do this!"

One week later, as Janet approaches the artist under the bridge, familiar blood-orange skies dance across the skyline. A dog rests by the artist's leg while he works diligently. He's painting the same VW van as in his previous work of art—Evelyn's van, which Norman stole. The van sits idle along the shoreline. This time, in his painting, a woman's body floats in the ocean background. Janet glances over the artist's shoulders, toward the ocean, and there, along the coastline, the van rests, and beyond the coastline, there is indeed a floating woman.

"Is that—" Janet can't bring herself to finish her statement.

"It is," says the artist.

Suddenly a *vrooom, screech!* sounds as the VW's engine revs and the tires burn, speeding off.

With a roar and a squeal, the van peels away, never to be seen again.

Book Club Topics & Questions for Discussion

Book Club Theme Ideas:

Funny mug gift exchange
Serve boozy coffee drinks
Serve sugar cream plantation pie
Serve Mountain Dew and champagne with Nilla Wafers

Questions:

Do you think Diana would have retired on her own if she had not been forced to resign from her position?

Theo believes that monsters are made; they're not born that way. Do you think people are born bad?

When Jeb and Diana agree to go on a date, their relationship seems quite natural, as if they were always meant to be together. Do you believe true love can be found after so many failed attempts?

When Diana is fired by her daughter, she experiences conflicting emotions. She feels both heartbroken and proud of her. Explain similar situations that arise in mother-daughter relationships in real life.

Filomena and Estelle both marry their high school sweethearts in the same year and later divorce them simultaneously. Twin relationships are unique. Do you think their relationship is healthy?

Carol, the nurse at The Ocean's Edge, works hard to care for the seniors, which can be quite challenging since she is a senior herself. Do you find it strange that when she falls ill and neglects her own self-care and well-being, no one inquires about her health or offers to help her?

Tom was not part of the group of seniors that helped solve cold cases. However, he suspected who might be murdering the residents. He shared his conspiracy theories with Carol, but she never passed along these suspicions to the group. Why?

Diana claims her memoir is too spicy for today's times. Do you believe she will publish it one day? Do you think anything is too spicy for today's times?

It seems that the police covered up Dennis's crimes. Do you believe some secrets should never be exposed? Why?

The retirees don't get the opportunity to read the entire journal, only the parts Bill reads out loud. If his friends were able to read the whole journal from the beginning to learn about his origin story, the killing of his dad, and his vigilante justice, would that change their overall opinion of him?

Do you think the retirees will continue pursuing cold cases? If so, will Jeb help?

Mr. Anderson communicates well with Carol, and Carol communicates effectively with other animals too. Do you believe that animals have a unique way of communicating with humans?

Theo believed that it was God's will for him to rid the Earth of its filth. Do you believe in vigilante justice? If so, under which circumstances?

Female murderers are rare, yet they are more common today than ever before. Are there more female serial killers? Or are women better at avoiding capture?

Theo creates a fictitious name for the journals. What do you suppose is the reason for this?

Estelle can talk to the dead. After Dennis dies, Estelle gives Carol a note from Dennis. Do you think Carol will share the meaning behind the note with her friends? Do you think Carol will ever tell them how Dennis died?

Theo collects lighthouses, which remind him of his childhood. What do you collect and why?

Bill found out that death row inmates have $40 to spend on their last meal. What would you order for your last meal?

Other Books by Leah Orr:

Murder Mystery Thrillers:

The She Shed

The Fruitcake

The Homecoming - Coming soon

Murder at the Opulence Hotel:

(Stand-alone stories within a series)

The Executive Suite (Book 1)

The Bartender (Book 2)

The Champagne Toast (Book 3)

Children's Books:

Goodnight, Molly

Messy Tessy

It Wasn't Me

Kyle's First Crush

Kyle's First Playdate

Summer Beach Fun - a coloring book for kids

Coming Soon . . .

The Homecoming

Homecoming queen Sofia Sheridan returns to Jensen Beach for her ten-year class reunion, filled with excitement and nostalgia. Her thrill quickly turns to terror when she discovers that three of her former friends from the homecoming court have been brutally murdered. Could she be the next target in this deadly game?

Keep in Touch

 facebook.com/leahorr

 instragram.com/leahorr723

 goodreads.com/author/show/
21341008.Leah_Orr

 https://www.amazon.com/stores/Leah-Orr/
author/B002BLWXFG

A Note from Leah

Dear Friends,

Thank you for reading *The Retirees* and spending time with some of the people in my head. I hope you enjoyed this twisty mystery and that these characters were as real to you as they are to me.

I would greatly appreciate it if you could take a moment to write a short review on social media and/or promote this book to your friends, family, and followers. Your support may introduce new readers to my books. I read every review, and since you took the time to write it, I make it a point to read it. I happily donate all profits from the sale of this book to the Cystic Fibrosis Foundation.

To keep in touch or inquire about discounted copies of this book for your book club or for signed copies, you can send an email to orrplace1@bellsouth.net or contact me through my website at www.leahorr.com. You can also follow me on Goodreads and Amazon.

With great gratitude,

Leah

Special Thanks

To Mr. Anderson, R.I.P., for inspiring me to tell portions of this story through his perspective. To the people who wrote me hate mail about foul language in some of my books, it inspired me to come up with creative ways for the characters at The Ocean's Edge to express their emotions using alternative language. Thank you to everyone who responded on Facebook's Jensen Beach Locals page for old-timey expressions to use within my story. Thank you, Marcia Dedert, for sharing your collection of lighthouses and allowing me to use this element in my story. A special thanks to my editor, Anna Roberts, who reads everything I write. The Ocean Breeze book club would like to thank Jane Hale for the inspiration behind *Murder on Maple*. Thank you to my daughter Camryn Orr, my alpha reader, for your keen eye and unique perspective. To my daughter Dr. Aly Orr, PsyD, for helping to indulge and motivate Theo's actions. To Bill McCord, for the inspiration behind one-eyed Bill, who was not originally part of the story —he bullied his way in, TBH, but wound up becoming one of my favorite characters. Now I can't imagine the story without him. Bill, I hope you enjoy my version of you as a *retiree*. What is it they say? Be careful becoming friends with a writer . . . you have little control over what tales they tell.

Cold Case Crime Stoppers

If you have information about a cold case murder along the Treasure Coast, please contact Treasure Coast Crime Stoppers at 1-800-273-TIPS.

To report information about a cold case from anywhere in the United States, please contact Crime Stoppers on the national Crime Stoppers tip line at 1-800-222-TIPS.

About The Author

Leah Orr is a #1 Amazon best-selling author. Her most popular book, *The She Shed*, has recently become a national bestseller. She lives with her husband and three daughters in Jensen Beach, Florida. Leah donates the profits from her books to the Cystic Fibrosis Foundation to help find a cure for her youngest daughter, Ashley, and other afflicted children.